VISIONS FROM THE

EDGE

SHORT STORIES

GAIL CURTIS

DEDICATION

To my wonderful family: Thank you for your humor, encouragement, love and support.

ACKNOWLEDGMENTS

To Barbara Beckley for assistance with editing

To Linda Edwards and Karen Brasier for editorial feedback

To Jacque, Kamara, and Alexis for their generous assistance

Special thanks to Brian Rouff and staff at Imagine Communications of Henderson, Nevada

TABLE OF CONTENTS

THE KEY

Jonathan Maples emerged from Number Fifteen Fremont Street in downtown San Francisco knowing that the carefully wrapped key in the pocket of his commuter shorts held both his destiny and demise.

Patting the hidden key was a ritual he'd performed at the end of every workday for several years. It was an obsessive-compulsive ritual: he knew it was there but had to constantly *know* it was there. It was always on his person when he was dressed and always within reach when he wasn't. The longstanding ritual was especially reassuring today.

Jonathan was relieved he would never spend another workday in the thirty-two-story glass skyscraper that had been his professional home for fifteen years. Or make the roughly twelve-mile walking commute to his home in Sausalito. He paused briefly before merging into the late afternoon throng of walking commuters now jammed into all lanes of Fremont Street. But not for one last glance at Number Fifteen. Or to watch the late afternoon sun reflect off of the gleaming glass structure. No. He had no nostalgia for Number Fifteen Fremont. Nor had he patience to wait for a break in the sea of walking masses rushing past him. Longing only for what was to come, Jonathan stepped boldly into the crush of pedestrians, cutting off a woman in the merge lane who was obviously irritated that his rudeness caused her to trip.

In the old commute-by-car days, such a blatant act would likely have triggered some idiot's road rage and Jonathan might be taking a bullet or club over the head about now. Mindful of people's frailties in that regard, he turned around to apologize to the woman he'd cut off, but was unable to find her in the crowd. Comforted that his back and head were safe from bullet and club, Jonathan pressed on, thankful for at least some of the zillion regulations they'd all come under since the turn of the 21st century.

He previously was allowed to quicken his commute by biking the first five miles from Fremont Street to the Presidio before walking over the Golden Gate Bridge and into Sausalito. However, those in his work category were restricted from bicycling a portion of the way or taking the ferry for the next two years.

The San Francisco Bay Area in 2050 was now a gunfree zone, notwithstanding the Constitution. As a result, the most that pedestrian commuters had to worry about for their infractions was a heated verbal exchange or a rare exchange of fisticuffs. However, except for the few regulations he deemed useful, Jonathan had been regulated to death.

Even before he began his professional career at Number Fifteen Fremont, most private vehicles had been banned from the Bay Area during business hours due to increasingly stringent federal clean air regulations. Later administrations eased many of those restrictions and once again allowed fossil fuels to power nearly half of the nation's cars. California authorities challenged the relaxed federal standards by instituting severe driving restrictions in the San Francisco area.

Middle-income Bay Area workers, who moved inland years ago to find affordable housing, were initially forced onto public transit, which they shared with underemployed and unemployed residents. These groups were often violent towards long distance commuters, resulting in a high rate of absenteeism. However, once commuters discovered there was safety in numbers and that the many could control or deter the errant few bad actors among them, the public transit commute became an accepted way of life.

Eventually, however, the Pedestrian Commute was devised and became mandatory. Jonathan and other Bay Area workers who lived within 10 miles of the San Francisco area were required to walk to and from their jobs, rain or shine. Many people worked from home or took time off during the heaviest winter rains.

City workers living in the inland and outlying regions were allowed to drive to within 50 miles of the city. From there they could take public transit, now fortified with increased security and citizens' patrols, and be transported en masse to within 10 miles of the city via ferry or motor coaches. The disabled, exempted from the regulation, were transported in and out of the city during commercial transport hours, with their work hours adjusted accordingly.

Settling into his commute, Jonathan's thoughts fast-forwarded to the present. He knew his decision would cost him everything he held dear: his wife Katherine, and their relatively happy marriage of 15 years, and their six-year-old fraternal twins, Mack and Mandy. He knew most people would think him insane to sacrifice a successful career and stable family life. Maybe he was. Could he be perfectly sane and still be aware he was about to commit an unthinkable act? He was as obsessive about the question as he was about his key ritual. The answer didn't matter. He'd simply come to the end.

Jonathan's spiritual disintegration had begun long ago. He was certain of that. Each unreasonable regulation imposed that was not challenged or resisted tore away a piece of his soul. He'd felt increasingly powerless to resist. Until now.

The minutia of it all relentlessly drained his spirit. Like dressing. He looked about at his fellow commuters with disdain, disgust, and dismay. *Sub-*California casual, he called it. The standard khaki slacks, commuter or athletic shorts, a company tee shirt or polo and the obligatory sneakers and socks. That was it to varying degrees.

Whatever had become of sophisticated, elegant business dressing? San Francisco certainly had the climate to support it. Not that shorts weren't attractive on a great pair of legs. He worked in a *sea* of legs, many of them made even firmer and shapelier from all the years of commuter walking and biking. What he missed was the mystery of wondering what kind of legs a flowing dress might conceal. Or the feeling he had when he wore a beautifully cut suit and stylish tie.

Most professionals kept an obligatory suit in their offices for business meetings, but Jonathan's time in such clothing was all too brief. Most of his workday, indeed much of his life, was spent in shorts. Everyone around him was in a similar state of undress. He would never be unfaithful to Katherine, but he missed seeing well-dressed women. And men.

But what bothered Jonathan most at the moment was the uncharacteristic humidity that had hung over the Bay Area the past several days without relief. He might as well balance a load of bricks on his head for the walk home—the air felt that heavy. He'd need even more of the tepid gray water sponges sold along the way.

How he hated those sponges! Even though he and all the other commuters relied on the sponges to make it through their daily trek, the sponges could not mitigate the stickiness of his clothing, however minimal, or the oppressive air. And he was thirsty, dammit! Really thirsty. Did anyone remember what it was like to totally quench one's thirst? He thought about it every day on his walk home.

Of course, everyone carried the ubiquitous thirst chips designed by a Sunnyvale biotech firm just after the turn of the century. Take one and the body's need for moisture was biologically and chemically sated. But for Jonathan, there simply was no substitute for thoroughly quenching his thirst with real water, as in the past. The gray water was potable and plentiful, but it was recycled from things most of them preferred not to think about.

Jonathan was surprised to see he was nearing the Golden Gate Bridge so soon. That meant he was entering the home stretch. Although he favored the quiet bridge lanes to the right for the walk home, he moved into one of the faster lanes by signaling with his raised left hand. No need to piss off another fellow commuter. He avoided the innermost lanes reserved for phone and computer users because he loved to enjoy the majesty of the bridge with as much quiet and solitude as he could manage among the multitudes.

In fact, Jonathan normally avoided looking at the runners in the fast lane or workaholics in the inner lanes. Doing so irritated him. But today he deliberately studied them, allowing the irritation to take root in his spirit and fester, as if needing fuel for the symbolic fire he was about to ignite.

Idiots, Jonathan thought, as he watched thousands of commuters still hammering away on all manner of keyboards and other work tools slung around their necks or waists and talking incessantly on their phones and into their devices. Was any of that work so important that it had to be done during a nearly twelve-mile trek after a long workday? Didn't they realize how ridiculous they looked? Was he the only one who saw the insanity of it all? Or was he the crazy one? Same questions. The answers, as always, were irrelevant.

Almost from the start, Jonathan had refused to take work home or work en route. What he did not accomplish at the office could wait until the next day. Surprisingly, that little act of defiance had been accepted by his superiors. After all, one oft-touted benefit of technology was that it would afford more leisure time. It seemed to him, however, that everyone worked increasingly more with each technological advance. What had become of his will to resist in other matters?

Once across the bridge Jonathan knew he would be ready for another thirst chip. Although Katherine kept him well stocked, Marin County homeowners along his route would be out as usual, encouraging commuters to walk across their once green yards. Lawns and flowers were prohibited as a result of the most recent drought and the once verdant Bay Area landscape was now as brown and barren as the hills of the California central valley in summer.

As a result, most homeowners posted signs on their property offering five thirst chips to each commuter who walked across their property. At this point in the commute the runners and power walkers had usually worked up a sweat and property owners were anxious for any amount of human perspiration to water their once green and colorful yards. Anything green growing in one's yard, even noxious weeds, was now considered a status symbol.

Because of the heavy air, Jonathan had already used all but one of the thirst chips Katherine had put in his shorts pockets that morning, and it would be another mile before he reached the first house offering the chips. He would have to buy a gray water sponge from one of the vendors whose makeshift carts lined the route. The thought reminded him of the plastic bottles of mineral water so popular at the turn of the century, now banned in favor of gray water. Residents of adequate means, however, maintained stashes of the bootleg mineral water for private consumption.

Forgetting about his growing thirst, Jonathan was overcome by guilt as he thought of Mandy and Mack, who loved to watch the daily pedestrian commute from their living room window. They'd climb onto the sofa in the front window and watch with anticipation for the first glimpse of their father among the commuters. Once they spotted him, Jonathan knew his twins would do as they always did—run to greet him with a fresh gray water sponge and a fruit-flavored thirst chip. Katherine would have a basin of cool gray water and chilled towels waiting for him the minute he came through the door.

He simply could not face his children today. Nor would he be able to face Katherine. His expression would give him away. He'd been too much of a coward to tell her, fearing she would try to talk him out of it. And she could have. Jonathan had never been an extremist or risk taker. He was predictable. Dutiful. Yet he knew he'd gone over the edge and it felt good. His children were not old enough to remember, let alone understand the step he was about to take. His wife would certainly remember. But like most people their age she had purposefully forgotten in order to exist in the new order.

"Daddy! Daddy!" Mack and Mandy screamed with glee upon seeing their father among the commuters. As expected, the children ran to their father with a sponge and thirst chip. Rather than take the sponge from them and release its liquid over his head and face as he usually did to their squeals of laughter, Jonathan avoided the delight in his children's eyes as he crouched down to hold and hug them both tighter than he ever had.

Leaving his children on the front porch to play, Jonathan paused before entering through the open front door to the family's modest bungalow. Once again he patted the pocket containing the key. Reassured for the umpteenth time it was there, he traced its outline with his fingers before carefully extracting from his shorts pocket the pouch that carried it. All he had to do was cross the living room before Katherine came out to greet him. Just a few more steps.

"Is that you, honey?" his wife called from the bathroom off the kitchen, where she had just placed chilled gray water washcloths on a towel stand for her husband. A watershed of guilt poured over Jonathan upon hearing his wife's voice. He realized she spoiled him as much as she could under the circumstances in order to make up for his long workday and commute. But he could not turn back now. "Pretty muggy walk home today, dear?" she added, not waiting for his reply.

Jonathan gingerly unwrapped the small gleaming silver skeleton key from the leather pouch that had housed it through the years. Katherine would be stunned to discover he still had it. Yet he'd secretly polished the slender key for the better part of fifteen years, as though by nurturing it he was tending something vital in himself.

"Jonathan is that you? Mack? Mandy?" Katherine called with alarm this time, dropping everything to check on the children.

Taking four stealth-like steps, Jonathan quietly crossed the small living room and inserted the key into the door of an adjacent room that had been locked since before the twins were born. Still unaware Jonathan was in the house, Katherine hurried from the bathroom through the living room towards the porch to look for the twins. Her footsteps froze, however, upon hearing the sound of a key being inserted into the door of the long-closed room. Forgetting about the twins momentarily— she'd heard their voices on the porch—she spun quickly toward her husband.

"Where did you get that key?" Katherine demanded, clearly alarmed. "What are you doing? Jonathan? Answer me! For God's sake, Jonathan, what are you doing?"

Jonathan sighed with relief as the key gingerly unlocked the door to the room. Slowly turning the doorknob with one hand, Jonathan closed his eyes like a lover anticipating a long-awaited kiss and flung the door open with such violence that it hit the wall behind it and sprung back toward him, stopping within inches of his temple.

Almost immediately a screeching, high-decibel alarm sounded along with a computerized voice that announced: "Violation in progress, authorities alerted! Violation in progress! Authorities alerted and en route. Stay clear! Stay clear!"

Startled but undaunted, Jonathan opened his eyes and looked quickly at the object of his long pent-up desire. If he correctly gauged the distance he could make it in one leap. Not daring to look at Katherine, barely even mindful of her presence, Jonathan leaped forward, fully clothed into his long unused shower stall and turned the water on full blast, not caring what might initially spew from the shower head. As long as it was wet and gave way to an avalanche of steamy, hot water. At first he was splattered with a thick coating of orange red sediment, which he slathered onto his hair like shampoo.

But when the first clear blast of hot water burst forth from the long shut down showerhead, Jonathan's spirit was overwhelmed like towns and cities downstream of a dam that has burst through its boundaries. Helpless in the face of it, he surrendered his entire being to the torrent of water. And although he had never cried in his life, his body was now overcome by gut-wrenching sobs of release.

In thinking of this moment over the years, Jonathan had always envisioned he would be able to recall the simple pleasure a long, hot shower once provided him. He did his best thinking in the shower. Mentally organized his day and thought out business strategy. Then too, there were the intimate, quiet times he and Katherine once enjoyed there. However, he didn't want to think, plan, or strategize now. He just needed to *be*.

Closing his eyes, Jonathan tilted his head back and opened his mouth to the flood of hot water, drinking it in until it made him choke and gag as it ran in rivulets down the sides of his mouth. He slowly closed his mouth, brought his chin toward his chest and slumped forward against the shower wall for support, allowing the water to pound his back and the back of his head, then flow down his legs into his socks and sneakers. He didn't have long now, but he was already free. The alarm immediately notified the water violation authorities, who had padlocked all showers years ago.

Jonathan had managed to keep his key. He'd also removed the shower door before it was padlocked so that he would not have to fight anyone to enter the stall itself once he unlocked the door to the shower room.

It would take authorities a few extra minutes to reach him since it was rush hour. In the interim, his neighbors were bound to make a citizens' arrest once the water violation alarm attached to each house sounded, alerting everyone that a water violation was in progress.

Katherine now screamed at her husband and tried to pull him out without entering the shower herself. She was frantic to get him out, as she could not appear to be a participant in her husband's madness. Her children would need a parent.

Ignoring his wife's pleas, Jonathan slowly peeled off his office tee, shorts, and briefs, but did not waste time removing his sneakers or socks. He straightened up momentarily to turn round and round mindlessly under the pulsating water before again slumping against the shower wall like a broken man. He let the water run through the rust-colored sediment in his hair, forming a red-orange trail down his back, across his buttocks and down his calves. His sneakers and socks were now burnt orange. He could no longer hear the wailing alarm or the computer voice exposing his crime to the community.

Almost too weak to stand, even with the shower wall for support, Jonathan placed one palm against the shower wall, hoping it would act like a suction cup and hold him up. Without looking, his other hand fumbled for the temperature control knob. Finding it, Jonathan made sure it was at the hottest setting. This was it! One of the many simple pleasures he'd been unable to forget—the tingle of almost burning hot water—*real* water, on his naked body. Even though this was the end for Jonathan, he felt fully alive.

Unable to reach Jonathan with her pleas, Katherine suddenly remembered the children and ran to gather them and lock the front door to stall the neighbors and authorities. But it was too late. Neighbors and commuters already filled her living room, her children in tow. Through the living room window, Katherine saw a S.W.A.T. team retrieve a straitjacket, handcuffs, and stretcher from a police van. Government utility workers were busy shutting off the remainder of the home's water system.

Katherine quickly pulled Mandy and Mack to her, trying not to alarm them. Her next-door neighbors, who were close friends, were already inside. Knowing they were there more out of curiosity and concern than civic duty, Katherine nudged her children towards them without a word and ran into the shower room, the multitudes on her heels.

"Let us at the selfish bastard!" they screamed. "Water violator!"

"Stay back!" Katherine roared, trying to push the door to the shower room shut against the weight of the crowd in her living room. No match for the merciless strangers pushing against the door, Katherine suddenly sensed the pressure against the door ease just as her strength began to ebb.

"Let us go in, ma'am," said one of the officers who had finally pushed through the throng of people in order to prevent mob justice.

"Please. Give me a few minutes with my husband," Katherine implored.

"You've got three," the officer replied, firmly closing the door to the shower room, leaving Katherine alone with her husband.

"Help me understand this, Jonathan," a frantic Katherine pleaded with her husband. "Couldn't you have talked to me? What will happen to us now? How will I take care of the children?" Katherine demanded, tears streaming down her face.

Jonathan, still sobbing, had slumped into a fetal position on the shower floor, the water still pouring onto his body as he wept into the drain. He heard his wife, even above the din of the crowd outside and the continuous shrieking of the alarm. He simply was unable to speak.

"Answer me, Jonathan!" Katherine demanded. "What will I tell our children? They're already here to take you, Jonathan. Talk to me. Please! Help me understand."

Katherine dropped to her knees on the floor outside the shower stall in defeat, burying her tear-streaked face in her hands.

Jonathan slowly looked up at Katherine from his fetal position. He wished he could tell her not to worry; that she and the children would be well taken care of. His eyes would have to convey the trust he needed her to have right now.

Slowly, Jonathan reached out and touched one of Katherine's hands. Startled, she uncovered her face at his touch and did not resist as he gently tugged at her hand and pulled her toward him. Relieved that he had finally responded, Katherine crawled into the shower and embraced her still sobbing husband. Slowly, Jonathan rose from his fetal position and sat on the shower stall floor, turning Katherine around so that she sat with her back to his chest, his arms encircling her. Tenderly, he tilted her head back toward him, exposing her face and chin fully to the now dwindling water stream. In doing so, he hoped she could feel some of what he felt, remember what he had never been able to forget. It was his way of saying both goodbye and that he was sorry. Words failed him but he was empty now. At peace. Clean.

Quietly the authorities entered the room, gently pried Katherine from her husband's embrace and removed Jonathan, naked except for his waterlogged sneakers and socks, from the shower stall. He would be transported to a psychiatric facility for observation, then to jail and eventually prison for violation of water regulations.

A few drops of water fell intermittently from the showerhead, even though the water was now shut off. After their father was straitjacketed and taken from the house, Mandy and Mack were allowed back inside. Still unaware of what had just happened, the twins wriggled their way through the now subdued crowd in the living room in an effort to see the source of the excitement. Upon seeing a shower stall for the first time their eyes were full of wonder, if not comprehension. Mack and Mandy quickly made a game of trying to catch the water droplets on their fingertips and the tips of their tongues.

THE FIRST TWENTY-FOUR HOURS

Natalie Thrift was the first child born to a Fifth Quadrant couple in five years and her mother was eager to get her home.

"Our daughter is exactly twelve hours old, Spence, and I want you to take us home," said a proud but tired Sarah Thrift to her husband, as she lay with their newborn daughter in one of the hospital's private birthing rooms. "Natalie's First Twenty-Four Hours Celebration is at two o'clock and I'd like to get her home and settled into the celebration chamber before all of our guests arrive."

"I know you're anxious to go home, darling," said Spencer, "but wouldn't you like to wait a while longer? The doctor wants to check both of you before you're released."

"I'm fine, Spence. Really. See if the nurse can have the doctor come by earlier so we can leave sooner. There's so much I want to do before her party."

"Don't worry about that," Spencer laughed, stroking Sarah's hair. "You're not going to do anything when we get home except rest. Besides, our families have been at the house since you went into labor early yesterday. I spoke with them last night. They told me the clock for her First Twenty-Four Hours Celebration is already up and running on the front lawn. They put it up at 6:00 p.m., right after she was born. And of course that signaled the neighbors to start the countdown by decorating our entire block. The city workers had the celebration chamber installed in our living room by nine o'clock. I'm told our little street is now something to see."

"I can't wait," said Sarah. An anxious glance at the wall clock facing her bed told her it was now 6:15 a.m. "But Spence, I don't want us to talk away our daughter's first twenty-four hours. Please. Take us home. This day is already going much too fast."

"If you hadn't insisted I bring nearly every clock from our house into the birthing center you wouldn't be so antsy," said Spencer, giving Sarah's hair a playful tousle as he got up from his chair to find the nurse. "Rest! That's an order, Sarah, or Natalie and I will attend her celebration without you."

"That's not funny," Sarah replied, clearly alarmed although she knew her husband was kidding.

"Sarah..." Spencer began, suddenly earnest as he turned back toward his wife before leaving the room.

"Yes, dear?" replied a distracted Sarah, still gazing at their infant daughter.

"Can we do this, Sarah? Can *you* do this? I just can't tell you how much you and Natalie mean to me, to our families...to everyone," he replied, unable to speak further.

"I know, honey," said Sarah, finally glancing up at her husband after hearing the tenderness in his voice. "We've waited a long time for this moment. Now that it's here I don't want to waste another precious moment of our daughter's first twenty-four hours. Now go. I promise I'll rest while you speak to the nurse."

After Spencer left the room, Sarah whispered to the tiny infant at her breast, "These are your first twenty-four hours my darling daughter. If I could stop time I would keep you in this moment forever."

The numerous clocks in her room indicated it was now 6:30 a.m. Not believing fifteen minutes had passed so quickly, Sarah glanced nervously at her wristwatch, hoping it would not confirm the other clocks. But her watch, like all the other clocks in the room, betrayed her hopes and confirmed it was indeed 6:30 a.m. A bedside clock/calendar indicated it was May 2, 2060. Drawing Natalie even closer, Sarah closed her eyes.

A short time later, as Spencer turned the couple's brand new family transport unit onto their narrow Fifth Quadrant street, the pleasant but boring symmetry of its government designed housing had been transformed into a whimsical, colorful children's paradise, all in Natalie's honor.

Twelve identical bungalows, different only in their freshly painted pastel exteriors, lined each side of the street. Each house was covered with flowers, streamers, and welcome banners. Strewn across each postage stamp-size lawn were pacifiers, baby shoes, baby bottles, and infant clothing. Each front yard housed a brand new children's swing set or play gym, all covered with garlands of flowers, ribbons and additional baby items.

Towering above all the decorations was the twelve-foot-tall First Twenty-Four Hours Celebration clock on the Thrifts' front lawn, which sat mid-block. A picture of Natalie was posted at the six o'clock numeral to mark the time of birth. Flower-covered clock hands indicated it was now 1:30 p.m. Despite the festive atmosphere, the street was deserted and Spencer and Sarah took advantage of the quiet to savor the moment.

"Look, Natalie," Sarah said, turning her daughter's tiny face toward the decorations, "this is all for you." Natalie opened her eyes briefly at the sound of Sarah's voice but immediately resumed her sound sleep.

The entire street was invited to celebrate Natalie's first twenty-four hours of life. Not that the other couples in their Quadrant had no children. All of them had at least one, including the Thrifts, but none of their children lived in the Fifth

Quadrant. Natalie would be considered the entire Quadrant's much beloved first newborn.

The Fifth Quadrant of the San Francisco Bay area had been Sarah and Spencer's government-mandated domicile since their first child, Adam, was two years old. Adam had lived in the Second Quadrant for the past five years and was now nearly seven. Not only would the Fifth Quadrant welcome the first child born there since the Quadrant was established in 2055, it would also welcome Adam as the only other child in the Quadrant.

The alarms on several of the clocks Spencer had packed in the back of the transport unit went off in unison, announcing it was 1:30 p.m. As if on cue, Sarah quickly glanced at her watch for confirmation.

"It's nearly time, dear. Shall we go in?"

As soon as Spencer gingerly maneuvered the transport unit into the couple's compact garage, their family members, who had been waiting in the house, exited through a rear door into the backyard. Sarah carried Natalie into the living room and immediately entered the celebration chamber. The chamber would protect both Sarah and Natalie from germs, and allow family and neighbors to enjoy the infant's first hours at close range from outside the chamber "bubble."

Once Sarah and Natalie were settled, family members re-entered the house in order to privately spend the next half hour with the couple and infant before the other guests arrived.

As soon as the First Twenty-Four Hours Celebration clock on the front lawn registered 2:00 p.m., the Thrift household began filling with neighbors and assorted Fifth Quadrant dignitaries and well-wishers.

Nearly seventy-five guests packed into the Thrifts' modest home for the celebration, and even three hours into the party none of them appeared anxious to leave. The celebration chamber was now cloudy with the fingerprints and handprints of Natalie's well-wishers. It was as if by touching the chamber, they could touch the infant herself. Sarah, who could speak with her guests via intercom, invited everyone to take as many photographs and videos as they wished until the party's official end at 6:00 p.m., marking the end of Natalie's first twenty-four hours.

Despite a difficult labor the day before, Sarah was actually energized by the festivities. Natalie slept through most of her celebration, which did not matter to anyone. Each couple on the block took turns opening their respective gifts for Natalie, so Sarah could admire them from inside the chamber. The baby now had more clothing, jewelry, collectibles, sports equipment, books, and games than she would be able to use for the next several years.

Throughout the celebration, many of the women wept tears of longing and celebration as Sarah breast-fed and rocked her daughter. Even when she changed the infant's diapers. At the same time, they were all careful not to mention Adam, since he would have a celebration of his own at the proper time. However, some of the men spoke quietly among themselves about Adam, their own absent children and their hopes for more children in the Quadrant.

As the gift giving continued, Sarah's eyes began to dart restlessly among the various clocks in the living room.

Spencer noted her growing distraction. His eyes conveyed the question each time he looked at his wife but she was now too preoccupied to notice. As the grandfather clock registered 5:45 p.m., Sarah again wished she could freeze her daughter's first twenty-four hours in that moment. The sound of the doorbell suddenly did just that.

Everything stopped—conversation, laughter, movement, and the rustle of wrapping paper— except the ticking of the countless clocks throughout the house. Spencer was closest to the door but did not move. His pleading face searched his wife's face for an answer—for reassurance. Instead, he was terrified by what he saw forming deep inside of her. He was as helpless in the face of it as she was powerless to stop its formation. In that moment he knew. Sarah was still resistant. The years of re-programming since Adam's removal had failed her.

"Don't answer it, Spencer," fear and bargaining now in Sarah's voice as tears rolled down her face.

"Sarah...don't...you mustn't...we can do this... please," Spencer urged, still frozen by helplessness and defeat.

"Don't...open...that...door!" Sarah commanded in a slow, guttural, deliberate tone, rage rising from the core of her being.

But the front door slowly opened from the outside as the pitch and volume of Sarah's voice rose. A thin brown-skinned Indian girl of about twelve, wearing a head muff and earplugs, stood cautiously in the doorway. Behind her stood a group of ten other children of various races and nationalities, all of them wearing the same earplugs. Although no one inside the house could see but Spencer, two other children were playing with the Thrifts' son Adam on the swing set in the couple's front yard.

The Indian girl stepped inside the living room, leaving the other children on the doorstep. After acknowledging Sarah and Spencer and others in the room, the child unfurled a scroll and announced the following:

> By Order of the State of California to Fifth Quadrant residents Spencer and Sarah Thrift: Your newborn daughter, Natalie Thrift, born May 1st in the year 2060, has

been declared a ward of the State and must now be given over into the State's care, to be raised in the Second Quadrant for the next five years. If, at that time, Sarah Thrift has uttered no further word or expression officially deemed offensive toward any racial, ethnic or religious group, or gender, then Natalie Thrift shall be returned home to the care of her parents.

"Get out of our home!" Sarah screamed, jumping out of her seat inside the celebration chamber and clutching Natalie with such ferocity that Spencer feared she would harm their daughter. But there was no escape and Sarah knew it. Once a mother and infant entered the celebration chamber, it was sealed throughout the festivities and could only be unsealed by government workers at the end of the celebration.

Spencer remained hopeful despite Sarah's outburst. She was certainly on dangerous ground but had not yet spoken any of the designated offensive words. Despite programming, it was now clear she still resented the modification to the Constitution's First Amendment decades earlier. This was his chance.

"Sarah, don't!" he again pleaded. "You can *think* what you want. You just can't *say* it. A violation is complete upon utterance. We'll still have Adam, darling. He's outside, Sarah. We'll at least have our son now. And Natalie will be returned to us later."

27

"I want that dirty little child out of our house—whatever she is—and all of those chinks, wetbacks, rednecks and niggers with her!" Sarah screamed, unleashing a pent up stream of poison and bitterness not uttered publicly by anyone in the Fifth Quadrant since its establishment. The children wore earplugs and were shielded from Sarah's torrent. However, anyone hearing such language was legally bound to report the offender.

The young girl continued the government edict:

> Natalie shall be raised among other children of all races, nationalities and religions, free of racial, ethnic and religious hostility in keeping with the State's policy in favor of diversity and zero tolerance for bigotry.

"Traitor! Traitor!" Sarah spat in Spencer's face as he gently wrestled Natalie from her grip once he was allowed inside the chamber. "How can you hand our child over to them?" The other Quadrant neighbors, as diverse as the children who arrived to claim Natalie, recoiled from the unfolding scene in horror. They had also lost their children due to offensive words uttered publicly by themselves or their children.

Now numb as the child continued reading the State's edict, Spencer felt a complete failure, even though it was his wife who uttered the offensive words that had cost them Adam, and now Natalie.

Because of Sarah's outburst, Adam would never be returned to them and Natalie was also gone forever. They'd initially lost Adam when he was only two after he called an Asian child in his First Quadrant daycare center a chink. By law, parents were held strictly liable for such remarks uttered by their children and automatically lost custody for five years. During that period the removed child was raised among children of all races, nationalities and religions and desensitized to the offensive remark.

The Fifth Quadrant had been established as a probationary zone for offenders deemed capable of rehabilitation, even a few of those deemed *Resistant,* like Sarah. Spencer could now legally denounce his wife and have her banished to the central valley to live among those officially declared *Intransigent.* But he would not do that. He still loved her and felt personally responsible for their loss, although no one would blame him.

If he stayed with her, the government would allow them to remain in the Fifth Quadrant for a brief period, but their neighbors, now afraid that association with the Thrifts would jeopardize reunification with their own children in the future, would shun them. The couple would need to move before any of their neighbors' children were returned to the Quadrant.

Remorse overwhelmed Spencer as he held his daughter tenderly before handing her over to the children. As the household clocks chimed 6:00 p.m., family and neighbors slowly filed out of the

Thrift household, some patting Spencer's shoulder in consolation as they left.

Sarah, now out of control with rage and grief, continued ranting obscenities but Spencer barely heard them. The damage was done. She could rant and rave until she was spent. He glanced out of his front window as though now in a bubble himself. In the yard he observed his son Adam, a big boy now, obviously happy, leaving with the children. Forever.

After the children were gone, Spencer was allowed to go outside. The street, which had seemed so colorful, jubilant, and hopeful only hours earlier, was now lifeless. Spencer touched the swing set in his front yard, which still swung back and forth from Adam's play there moments earlier. The newly purchased swing sets in his neighbors' yards were as motionless now as they were when they'd returned home from the birthing center, their colorful streamers and banners torn down in anguish, mourning, and disgust.

As Spencer sat in the swing set intended for his children, he and the neighbors who peered at him through tightly drawn curtains and blinds, watched as the hope born earlier that day was slowly smothered by the stultifying symmetry of their Fifth Quadrant street.

BUD 'N' PATCH

"Patch hears the grass patrol helicopter approaching overhead, Bud. Can you let him outside?" Courtney asked her husband as they prepared coffee and their favorite weekend breakfast.

"Another peaceful Saturday morning in my own backyard ruined," Bud complained, not trying to hide his sarcasm. "Until the grass patrol leaves the area Patch doesn't need to go out. He can wait in here with us. Besides, he makes such a fuss the pilot hovers even lower over our yard when he spots him."

"He's only playing with him, hon," Courtney countered, trying to calm her irritated husband. "Besides," she continued, "it's Patch's weekly entertainment. The patrol won't last long and who has grass anymore, anyway?"

"Well, no one of course. We desert dwellers haven't had grass for a while now. Hard to believe we once actually had the option of keeping our lawns or converting them to desert landscaping, without grass of course."

"True," Courtney agreed. "And we opted to keep our grass. I still can't believe it was later outlawed here in Las Vegas," she concluded. "When was that Bud, about 2050 or so?"

"I can't remember now. It's been at least 10 years. Amazing. We're in the latter half of the twenty-first century and green grass is illegal. I just don't get it. We got past the drought several years ago—just like California did years earlier. Our state's water stores are up and we've negotiated adequate water supplies with neighboring states. You'd think that would justify a few patches of green grass for us to enjoy."

"Obviously not."

"Well, we lost the grass," Bud grumbled, "but gained these intrusive, weekly patrols that ruin the sanctity of my quiet Saturday mornings in the backyard with Patch and my newspaper. Maybe if I keep Patch inside today the pilot will fly right past our desert oasis of rocks and shrubs and leave us alone. Me and Patch can go outside then."

"But in the meantime," Courtney interrupted, "all of this racket is driving me crazy—Patch's incessant barking to go outside and the helicopter overhead. Something's gotta give or I will!

"Besides," she continued, "do they think anyone would have the nerve to plant grass when the government patrols weekly for any sign of it growing in our yards? It's a crime now for God's sake and there's no fine anymore, only mandatory jail time.

For grass! We've adjusted to the artificial turf in the parks but Patch doesn't even like to go there anymore. And the grass-scented pee pads the government installed in the dog parks were not a winner."

"Down Patch, down boy. Quiet!" Bud admonished his excited five-year-old beagle.

"If you're not going to let him out, then take him out of here at least," Courtney pleaded. "Maybe to your study. Anywhere, just out of here. I can't take the racket."

"I'll take him down to the basement then."

"Downstairs? But honey, it's such a beautiful day. Can't you two stay above ground with me?"

"Well, that's certainly my plan," Bud teased.

"You know what I mean," Courtney replied, not at all amused. "You know I can't go down there. And if you go downstairs you'll start tinkering and I won't see you for hours."

"We won't be down there long. I promise. Besides, Patch will need to come up soon to go outside. You want him quiet? He'll be quiet in the basement. He always is. Why don't you join us? I'll carry you down."

"Thanks, but no thanks. No desire to be a basement dweller on such a beautiful day. Jesus. The patrol is still over our house. Please, either send Patch outside or take him downstairs. I can't take the noise."

"C'mon, Patch boy. Let's leave mamma here and go to our lair."

"All right, desert me then. You too, Patch."

Courtney had Parkinson's disease. Although she had fair mobility she was unable to negotiate stairs, and they had agreed she would not attempt it anymore on her own. They lived in a one-story house, save for the basement, which was rare in their part of southern Nevada. Bud agreed to clean the basement and Courtney hadn't minded, as Bud was very organized and a bit of a neatnik.

"Before you go honey, listen. Patch is not outside and the helicopter sounds like it's stationary, right above our house. Sure we can't send Patch out so the patrol can move on? Maybe they're waiting for him to come outside."

"No. Our fault for allowing it to continue for so long. Let's just ride it out. I don't want what used to be my peaceful Saturday morning in the backyard to continue to be a game between Patch and the patrol pilots. The sooner they pass over the better."

"But that's just it," Courtney countered. "They're not passing over, even with Patch inside."

The couple was unaware that during the previous night the government had carried out a stealth air patrol over their neighborhood. The night patrols were random and never announced, employing quiet aircraft, sometimes drones. The patrols focused on grass as well as clandestine marijuana growing operations. Recreational marijuana was now legal but the state government controlled its growth, distribution, and sale. It was the headline-making bust of an illegal grow house next door to their former house that brought Courtney and Bud to this area several years before.

The night patrol had noted an unusual beam of light emanating from the top of the couple's roof. As a result the weekend patrol pilot received orders to conduct a thorough observation over the house and yard the following day. It would be nearly impossible to catch a beam of light in the desert sunshine, but the pilot had his orders to give the yard extra scrutiny.

"There's nothing for them to see here," said Bud. "They should just move on."

When, he mused, would the government stop enacting measures that encroached upon people's privacy? He knew water conservation was important but so were people's simple pleasures.

Had lawmakers forgotten how important grass was to the environment? How much people and animals enjoyed it?

Until their favorite neighborhood park was stripped of grass, Bud had enjoyed driving past it on his way home from work. The park was beautifully maintained and driving past the long expanse of green grass lifted the day's stresses as he approached home. He often stopped and walked the length of the park barefoot. Even if the outside temperature was soaring, the temperature along the park was noticeably cooler.

Several years ago, when Parkinson's had not yet affected Courtney's gait, a perfect weekend for the couple included a walk to this park and the adjacent dog park. However, the dog parks were essentially neutered after grass was outlawed in residential yards and the parks stripped of grass, leaving dogs to negotiate the rocky native soil. When dog owners complained, the government removed some of the larger rocks and hauled in a more uniform gravel.

Dispensers with biodegradable grass-scented pee pads were also installed in the years that followed. However as use of the dog parks continued to decline, they were eventually shuttered. Dogs now had a small gravel section with dispensers in a designated section of each public park. Some public parks had artificial green turf but most had gravel. As a result, the family's weekly walk to the park became less enjoyable for them and less social for Patch. Once Courtney's gait worsened, they ceased their walks to the park with Patch altogether.

Bud hadn't forgotten the coolness of grass fresh with morning dew or the feel of it between his toes. Patch was bred by a family in northern Nevada, which still allowed grass in some areas. He didn't want Patch to forget what it felt like to run, play and roll around in the grass. What did it do to a species when it was denied such a natural part of its environment?

His first date with Courtney was a picnic he arranged at the park they now avoided. They shared it on a hand-painted blanket Courtney supplied for the occasion. They didn't have Patch yet. He came along after the couple was married, but Courtney brought Chloe, a shih tzu puppy she had at the time.

As Bud placed Courtney's blanket on the grass and laid out the picnic spread, she was impressed that he also included snacks, water, and a toy for Chloe. Nearly two years after that first date they were married in the same park, surrounded by a small group of family and friends and, of course, Chloe.

They continued to enjoy the park with Chloe after they were married and then with their boxer Ferdinand after Chloe passed away. But as Courtney began losing mobility and the parks their grass, she and Bud opted for shorter strolls closer to the house.

On this particular morning, the moment Bud and Patch left the kitchen for the basement the doorbell rang, which triggered Patch's renewed barking. Not expecting anyone so early on a Saturday, Courtney called downstairs to Bud to come up and answer the door. It took a few calls, each louder than the last, before Bud finally responded.

"Yes, hon?"

"Someone's at the door, Bud. Can you come up?"

"Be right there. C'mon Patch. Our damsel needs us."

Once upstairs, Bud passed by Courtney in the kitchen and entered the living room where he opened the front door. A stranger he could not see well stood on the other side of the metal screen door.

"Morning. Can I help you?" Patch continued to bark and jump up and down. "Down Patch, down boy," Bud commanded, still peering through the screen.

"Morning. Mr. Larsen? I'm Officer Dansen from the civil air patrol. I'm the pilot who normally flies the weekly patrol in your area, but I'm not flying today. That's my partner making all of that racket over your house right now. I recognize your little guy right there—he always jumps up and down when he sees my chopper."

"So you're the one. How can I help you?"

"I'm sorry Mr. Larsen but following last night's air patrol a warrant was issued to search your premises."

"What? Why for Pete's sake?" Bud demanded. "You can see there's not a blade of green grass in our yard and this certainly is not a marijuana grow house—we moved here to get away from one in our old neighborhood. We're law abiding citizens, dammit!"

"What is it, honey?" Courtney called from the kitchen, alarmed after hearing Bud's raised voice at the door.

"It's the civil air patrol, honey. The officer here has a warrant to search the premises."

"What? That can't be! Anyone can see we don't have grass or marijuana in the yard. Why us? Why our house?"

"I can't tell you that sir, ma'am," the officer replied. "We won't be coming in with a SWAT team or anything like that, and you have the right to inspect the warrant before I enter. Please unlock the screen.

"Also, records indicate you have two registered firearms on the premises. Please place them, unloaded, on any table in the room you're in with the registration paperwork. We'll verify your firearms against our paperwork. Any unregistered weapons located during our search will be confiscated. You can inquire about registering them at the local police station later after paying any fines.

"Once the guns are in place, please step outside and secure your dog. My partner and I will then begin our search. I estimate it will not take more than an hour. We will not look through any files— just a general check of the premises is all."

While Courtney remained with Patch, who was now leashed, Bud retrieved the couple's guns and registration papers and placed them within eyesight of Officer Dansen, who was now joined by another officer.

"Okay, we're ready to step out," said Bud.

"All right," Dansen replied. "While you're securing the dog, the helicopter overhead will circle the block once and return. He'll remain pretty much over your house until we're done."

"Government intrusiveness at its best!" Bud muttered under his breath. "I'm sure the neighbors are gawking, waiting for us to be hauled out in handcuffs."

"I'm sure everything will be fine, Mr. Larsen," Dansen replied. "I'm just doing my job."

"Sorry I can't be more welcoming," said Bud. "Me and Patch here used to enjoy our quiet Saturday mornings in the backyard. Now we have the government patrolling over our yard every week looking for some goddammed grass! C'mon Patch, let's go outside boy."

"Hey there little fella," Dansen greeted Patch. Wary that his masters were leaving the house and two strangers going in, Patch stopped barking but did not respond to the officer's greeting.

The air patrol's search of the couple's home took only half an hour. The officers looked through the couple's three-bedroom, two-and-a-half-bath home, including the basement. Afterward the officers did a cursory walk around the outside of the house before returning to the front door. Bud and Courtney remained outside during the search—

Bud seething and Courtney confused. Patch resumed barking when the helicopter returned and remained stationary over the house. However, this time Patch's barking reflected Bud and Courtney's anxiety.

"Mr. and Mrs. Larsen, we're done and have given the pilot an all clear. You're free to re-enter the house and secure your weapons."

Bud opened the door, not trying to hide his disgust.

"Well?"

"We're not allowed to give you an official report at this stage. You'll get a letter of finding within two weeks. But unofficially, I'll say we found nothing amiss. Sorry for the intrusion. Hope you'll enjoy the rest of your day. I must say that Patch's greeting every Saturday when I fly over is a highlight of what's typically a boring patrol.

"Also, I've gotta say you have one of the neatest basements I've ever seen. You make my garage man cave look like the sty my wife says it is. By the way, beautiful hallway floor. Is it glass?"

"Yes. Glass cinderblock. I hand-painted it," Courtney replied.

"Impressive," said Dansen. "We're out folks."

"What the hell, Bud?" Courtney exploded after the officers were gone. "I'm mortified! What must our neighbors think?"

"Who cares?" Bud replied. "Privacy is a thing of the past."

"But why us, honey? I mean we couldn't be more law abiding."

"That's what I told 'em. But I'm sure they hear those famous last words every time they get ready to inspect."

"Well, thank God we're cleared."

"Unofficially at least."

"Well, I'll take "unofficially" until we get the letter," said Courtney. "You know what else?"

"Pray tell."

"Think I've had enough excitement for the morning."

"That makes three of us," said Bud, hugging Patch and detaching his leash. "Now that the helicopter has gone I'm gonna let Patch out in the back for now. I'm sure the neighbors are still out front and I'm not up for a walk."

"I understand."

"Besides," Bud continued, "we don't owe them an explanation. "If you don't mind, think I'll return to the basement for a while to chill out."

"Sounds like a good idea, sweetheart. Think I'll paint for a while. Afterward we can have lunch, then maybe sit outside for a bit and enjoy a glass of wine. It's so beautiful out.

"Makes me think of our picnics in the park back in the day."

"Don't remind me," said Bud, still clearly upset by the morning's events. Courtney gave him a quick kiss before she left the living room for her painting studio in one of the converted bedrooms.

"I'm gonna brew fresh coffee," Bud called after her. "Would you like me to bring you a cup when it's ready?"

"No thanks, Bud. No appetite for anything right now. I'll paint for a while. Then I'll call you and Patch to come up for lunch. Maybe we'll both feel like eating then. We never got to eat our breakfast."

As Courtney headed to her studio, Bud let Patch out into the backyard from a door in the kitchen and began making coffee to take downstairs.

Unfortunately there wasn't a single project he felt like working on after the morning's events. Grief overwhelmed him as he watched Patch make his way through the desert landscape outside to relieve himself. It had been a helluva day so far.

Once Patch was back indoors, Bud took his freshly brewed coffee and headed to the basement. Rather than start a project and let the coffee get cold, he decided to just sit and enjoy the entire cup before beginning. Patch sat at his feet. He was still unsettled by the morning's events, however, and none of his projects interested him.

After finishing his coffee Bud returned to the kitchen for another cup, Patch in tow. Once there he didn't really want more coffee so he busied himself in the kitchen tidying up their unfinished breakfast and making a few trips back and forth to the basement. On his last trip downstairs, he decided to just sit and think. Patch took a nap. Bud also dozed off until he was awakened by Courtney's voice calling him from the kitchen.

"Bud? Are you and Patch ready for lunch?"

"I think so, dear. Guess me and Patch dozed off for a bit."

"And all the time I was in my studio I thought you were working away down there," Courtney teased.

"I just couldn't get my mind into any of my projects."

"Well, what do you want for lunch?"

"I'm not sure. I'll be right up and we can figure it out. C'mon boy. Time for you to go outside again, then lunch. Let's go up." As soon as they reached the kitchen, Patch ran to the door and Courtney let him outside.

"What do you feel like today? Sandwich? Leftovers?"

"I'm not really very hungry although I could eat. This morning just drained me."

"Me too. I don't have much of an appetite either, but we probably need to eat because breakfast was interrupted."

"Since neither of us is that hungry, feel like just talking for a bit?"

"Of course not," Courtney replied with a slight laugh. "But that's usually my line."

"Do you mind talking downstairs? I don't feel comfortable up here after this morning."

"If you're willing to carry me downstairs into your sanctuary, I suppose we can have a cellar chat. Let me get Patch in first." She opened the kitchen door and called to Patch. "C'mon, boy. Your papa has invited me to the basement manor."

"Ready to be swept off your feet?"

"As only you can do, my love!"

Bud lifted Courtney and carried her down the stairs to the basement, Patch following.

"I'm impressed, Bud. Now I see why the officer complimented you on the basement. It's meticulous."

"Surely you wouldn't expect anything less from me. Let's sit here in these chairs."

Bud placed Courtney in a standing position. Once she was certain of her balance, she sat down in an easy chair next to Bud's. Patch, apparently happy to have Courtney in the basement, ran from her to Bud, then to Bud's work console and back to Courtney.

"I need to come down here more often, boy," Courtney said to Patch. "I'm getting quite a welcome."

"I was hoping you would say that," said Bud. "You're always welcome down here. We can still have a stairlift installed for you."

"Nope. Don't want one. This is your cave—and Patch's—and I have mine. I have no need to come down here. Besides, she said smiling, it was fun being carried over the cellar threshold by my strong hubby."

"This morning really got to me, babe," said Bud.

"I know. Who could have imagined only a few years ago that government helicopters would patrol for green grass? And that our houses could be searched on suspicion of having it? Well, actually we weren't told why they searched."

"I hate the intrusion into our home and the decreasing options we have to enjoy nature."

Bud slowly rose from his chair and approached his work console.

"Oh no. You invite me down for a chat, and then decide to work at your console. Think that's my cue to go back upstairs and start lunch."

Bud did not immediately respond. Patch followed Bud to the console but turned to look at Courtney.

"Wha...what's happening?" Courtney looked at Bud with alarm then back to his console in amazement. Bud quietly walked over to Courtney and took her hand, pulling her up gently from the chair. Suddenly Patch went crazy with excitement as Bud's work console opened in the middle and slid into pocket openings on either side.

Not letting go of her hand, Bud walked Courtney into a sunny, verdant park with the most beautiful, meticulous green lawn she had ever seen. In the center of the lawn sat the picnic basket from their first date, on top of the blanket she hand painted years earlier. Next to the basket was a bottle of wine and two wine glasses. Patch had a water dish and bowl of food. There were even framed pictures of Chloe and Ferdinand.

"I can't believe it, Bud. How long has this been here?"

"Longer than I care to admit."

"But you were so indignant with the officer."

He smiled, slyly. "I was good wasn't I?"

As Courtney continued to take it all in, Patch took off across the lawn and rolled over and over on the grass.

"Oh my God, Bud, we *are* criminals!"

"No, I am. That's why I never told you, in case we were ever caught."

"Something obviously tipped the government off but the patrol officers obviously didn't find this," said Courtney.

"No, they wouldn't. But I was a bit careless and my carelessness brought them here."

"What did you do?"

"It's what I didn't do. I forgot to activate the wood subfloor that I installed under the glass block floor in our hallway upstairs."

"Is that why you wanted a glass floor and asked me to paint it?"

"To be honest, yes. But I really *do* like your painting."

"Makes me wonder now," Courtney laughed. "But hasn't our water use skyrocketed? Maybe that brought them here."

"I don't think so. I pulled out some of our shrubs, added even more rock, and diverted the water. Besides, the officers could not see through the glass floor anyway because it's block glass, but the painting you did on it and the wood subfloor underneath were additional safeguards. The skylight above the hallway allows the sun to go right through the glass hallway floor to our private "park" here during the day. Sometimes at night I leave an artificial light on in here.

"As long as the wood subfloor is closed under the glass floor, sunlight won't come through. The officers today didn't mention anything, but when they saw the skylight they probably figured that any light coming from our house at night was probably a hallway light. Thank goodness I went to the basement when I did this morning. I'd forgotten to deploy the wood subfloor under the hallway glass floor."

"Just look at our Patch. He's having the time of his life," said Courtney.

"I know. I think I did this as much for him as for me."

"And what about me?" Courtney teased.

"Look at the sign there," said Bud, directing Courtney's attention to a plaque at the entrance. It read, "Courtney's Park."

"Oh Bud," Courtney gasped. "I don't know what to say. Thank you sweetheart—a park of our own. And with real green grass! I guess we're grass growers after all," she said smiling, as Bud opened the wine and Patch ran and rolled with abandon.

"Bud 'n' Patch. My boys."

VISIONS FROM THE EDGE

ENDANGERED

Momentum had been growing around the U.S. Supreme Court building in the nation's capital for days. In an unprecedented move, the Court allowed those awaiting a much-anticipated argument regarding endangered species to camp in the area surrounding the Court building itself. The justices also allowed video monitors installed outside so that those unable to sit inside for oral arguments could watch the arguments in their entirety.

Campers continued to stream into the District of Columbia on this morning, joining the earliest attendees who arrived the previous week. Visitors to the nation's capital, as well as local residents, had all manner of pets in tow: canine, feline, equine, and porcine, with rodents and reptiles generously represented. In addition, still more animals were represented in photos and posters and depicted on attendees' clothing.

Health officials in the District of Columbia were unprepared for the number of people and animals arriving. However, attendees quickly organized themselves and partnered with health officials to keep themselves and their animals clean and the area cleared of animal and human waste and trash.

Plaintiffs' attorneys Elizabeth Bay and Ned Sumner paused on the courthouse steps to take it all in. They were surprised that an endangered species case would generate such a turnout.

"I can't believe our case brought out all these folks — and their animals," Liz remarked.

"Neither can I," Ned replied. "It's such a beautiful day. I'd like to be out there with my dogs. We could use a day in the sun."

In the seventy years preceding this case, animal rights activists flooded the lower courts with cases seeking to protect even the most obscure species and, sometimes, to expand the list of endangered species and protections given them. The nation's highest Court had entertained a limited number of endangered species cases but sent most of them back to the lower courts for disposition.

However, the Court's handling of this case continued to draw criticism from the legal community, constitutional scholars in particular, and threatened a showdown with Congress for allegedly exceeding its jurisdiction. The most serious criticisms were that the Court, in taking this case immediately after it was filed in the lower courts, not only exceeded its jurisdiction but was also becoming an activist Court.

The justices learned of the case's anticipated filing beforehand and intervened in the filing

52

process, arguably without authority. The Court ordered that the case be filed under seal, and imposed a gag order on both sides until the matter was briefed and oral argument was scheduled and held. Congressional furor over the Court's intervention was immediate.

Although the U.S. still retained three branches of government in 2040, the branches were no longer equal in actual *practice.* The aftermath of presidential elections some years earlier had put the nation on an authoritarian path that, fortunately for the nation, the military did not wholly support. So grave was the peril, however, that the Supreme Court justices managed to put aside the partisanship of their respective appointments and uphold what remained of the Constitution as best they could.

Ironically, they did so on occasion by acting outside of their authority. When Congress failed to act or abdicated its lawmaking role in key areas, the Court sometimes *made* law, especially if it pulled the nation back from outright dictatorship.

Rumors were rife about the endangered species case. The public knew little about the nature of the case or the endangered species involved. There was speculation that a recently discovered marine species was involved. The long-awaited oral argument was scheduled to begin within the hour.

Court security and staff began seating the limited number of spectators who would be allowed inside. Each person granted entry would hear ten minutes of argument before being ushered out to allow another group of visitors inside. The justices were firm about not allowing animals in the courtroom.

Campers and others in attendance now numbered at least 100,000. Inaugural level security measures were in effect outside the building. Supreme Court police estimated at least 50,000 animals present. Despite the highest-level security, the multitudes and creatures in tow enjoyed a festive, peaceful gathering.

"I'm still smoldering around the edges from our last argument in here, Liz," Ned commented as they entered the court building.

"Why the pessimism? We don't even have that decision yet."

"Because you like to tilt at windmills."

"If we go down in flames, it won't be the first time. Besides, we might win that last case."

"Judging from the justices' questions, I doubt it."

"I know you have my back, but thank goodness I'm lead counsel on this one," Liz laughed, as they entered the courthouse doors.

Liz and Ned had been law partners in their own civil litigation firm the past twenty years. Each had argued a fair number of cases before the Supreme Court. Several years ago they began taking two pro bono cases a year and today's endangered species case was one of them. Liz knew Ned was reluctant to accept this case. It was her year to select the cases, however, and he had acquiesced. Because of his reticence, Liz agreed to be lead counsel.

Now seated at plaintiffs' table in the courtroom, Liz could not believe she was back before the Supreme Court on another pro bono case only six months after arguing the last one. She remembered the phone call that brought this case to her attention shortly after the last one concluded.

"This is Garrett, Liz," said the voice on her office phone.

"Garrett Granger!" she replied, happy to hear from her old friend. "How are things in the rarified air of tax law these days?"

"Taxing."

"I made that one easy for you, didn't I?"

"You did."

"Shall we start over? How are you?"

"Next time we have coffee, I'll tell you in detail. For now, however, I have a pro bono case for you. It's *Tennessee Valley Authority v. Hill*, a U.S. Supreme Court case." [1]

"You don't mess around do you?" Liz asked, laughing. "What's this about, Garrett?"

"It's an endangered species case."

"Not my area of expertise. You know that."

---

[1] Tennessee Valley Authority v. Hill, 437 U.S. 153 (1978).

"This case has your name written all over it. Just read it and get back to me."

"You know that Ned and I just concluded a pro bono case a few months ago. We're exhausted, way behind on our regular caseload, and have no time—repeat no time—to take on another one right now."

"I understand. Just promise me you'll read it and get back to me."

"That I can do. Talk to you soon."

"Thanks, Liz. You know I wouldn't ask if it weren't important."

Liz read the case as soon as she hung up and immediately called Garrett back.

"Okay, so what gives? Again, this is not my area. Even if I was interested, I don't think the political climate is favorable for an endangered species case. In fact I'd say the climate is downright hostile. You've seen how all of the environmental protections put in place by earlier administrations have been nixed by the last few administrations."

"Look, Liz, if you could take on the last pro bono case you just argued, this one will be a walk in the park."

"The only walk in the park I'll agree to at the moment is one with you, the park near my office, tomorrow bright and early. Coffee is on you by the way."

"Only coffee? I'd spring for lunch if you insisted."

"I despise working lunches and dinners so you lucked out this time."

Six months earlier Liz and Ned had argued the pro bono case of *American Citizens v. United States* before the Supreme Court. [2] That case was filed on behalf of all U.S. citizens and persons within its borders. The attorneys argued that plaintiffs' rights of life, liberty and the pursuit of happiness, set forth in the preamble to the Declaration of Independence, were jeopardized by record gun deaths from ever increasing mass shootings, homicides, and endemic gun violence in general. A brief submitted in that case by the nation's health authorities noted that America's level of gun violence, and effects therefrom, constituted a national health crisis.

Additionally, the nation's mental health experts submitted briefs in support of plaintiffs, which concluded the nation suffered palpable malaise from unchecked gun violence. The lawsuit sought a finding by the Supreme Court that Americans' rights to life, liberty and the pursuit of happiness were at odds with ever increasing gun violence and that Congress *must act* to protect citizens' rights.

The earlier lawsuit did not seek to overturn the Second Amendment. Litigation to amend or abolish the Second Amendment was already working its way through the lower courts. The San Francisco Bay area had already been granted a gun ban on

---

[2] American Citizens v. U.S. is a fictional case for purposes of this story.

limited grounds in one of the cases. Even though the Second Amendment withstood that court challenge, the Bay area now had a number of gun-free zones.

"Here we go," Ned whispered to Liz at counsel table, interrupting her thoughts about their recent case. Needless to say she'd taken that walk in the park with Garrett and was about to argue the case he brought to her attention. The court's marshal stepped forward to begin proceedings.

"The Honorable, the Chief Justice and the Associate Justices of the Supreme Court of the United States. Oyez! Oyez! Oyez! All persons having business before the Honorable, the Supreme Court of the United States are admonished to draw near and give their attention, for the Court is now sitting. God save the United States and this Honorable Court."

Amen, Liz thought.

Liz and Ned stood at plaintiffs' table facing the justices' chairs. U.S. Solicitor General James Paul stood at the government's table across the aisle. Spectators were not allowed to talk inside the Courtroom but the chamber was loud with anticipation. Outside the Court the crowd suddenly quieted as the justices entered in a single file and took their seats. Chief Justice Taylor, appointed to the bench nearly 10 years earlier, began the proceedings.

"Good morning, counsel."

"Good morning Chief Justice, your honors," returned the attorneys.

"You may be seated," the marshal directed, nodding at visitors. "I believe all counsel are present."

"That's correct," responded Solicitor Paul, stating his appearance for the record.

"Elizabeth Bay and Ned Sumner present on behalf of plaintiffs," Liz announced. "Mr. Chief Justice, and May it please the Court, we request leave to have our clients brought into the courtroom."

Many of the spectators were caught off guard by her request to have the species present.

"The justices have determined there is no threat to anyone here today from the species at issue," Chief Justice Taylor replied. "Therefore the species shall be brought in shortly. We've read your briefs. You may make your record, Ms. Bay. I understand you are lead counsel?"

"That's correct," Liz replied, approaching the podium. "We request a finding and declaration that the plaintiffs constitute an endangered species. As such, plaintiffs seek the same protections heretofore granted other endangered species under the *Endangered Species Act*. This is an issue of first impression we believe is ripe for review."

"Thank you for your brevity, Ms. Bay, given that you and Mr. Sumner submitted voluminous briefs.

However I don't find clear authority for your position therein."

"Exactly!" declared Solicitor Paul, rising to address the Court.

"I should not have to remind you, Mr. Paul, that civility and professionalism are paramount here. Ms. Bay I'd like you to address the authority for your proposition. The government may then respond."

After an uncomfortable silence, Liz replied: "I have no legal authority directly on point, your honor."

Ned heard several of the spectators gasp at his partner's response. He was not surprised. Even laypersons could surmise that no attorney wanted to tell the U.S. Supreme Court that he or she had no legal authority for an argument. Liz had done just that and he knew his partner relished the shock that registered in the courtroom.

"We believe, however," Liz continued undaunted, "that the *Endangered Species Act* of 1973 best supports our position." [3,4] In 1978, this very Court found in the case of *Tennessee Valley Authority v. Hill* that—quoting in part here—"[t] he plain intent of Congress in enacting" the Endangered Species

---

[3] <u>Endangered Species Act of 1973</u>, 16 U.S.C. §1531 (1973).

[4] The author's interpretation of the *Endangered Species Act* is fictional for purposes of this story.

Act "was to halt and reverse the trend toward species extinction, whatever the cost." [5],[6]

And, as we explained in our briefs, that case involved a tiny fish discovered in 1973 called the snail darter, that held up completion of the TVA's nearly completed Tellico Dam Project. Plaintiffs in this case are at least as deserving of protection under the *Endangered Species Act* as the snail darter."

"Solicitor Paul?" the Chief Justice directed.

"First, the government contends the complaint is overbroad. Second, plaintiffs' attorneys concede they have no legal authority directly on point. Third, even though the Endangered Species Act of 1973 remains the controlling authority on endangered species, the government sees no rational way plaintiffs can place themselves within its protections."

"Ms. Bay?"

"As we've pointed out in our briefs, in order to petition for listing under the *Endangered Species Act*, the species seeking protection must meet one of the following five criteria, which I'll paraphrase:

1. The present or threatened destruction, modification, or curtailment of its habitat or range

---

[5] TVA v. Hill, 437 U.S. 153 at 184.

[6] The author's interpretation of *TVA v. Hill* is fictional for purposes of this story.

2. Over-utilization for commercial, recreational, scientific or education purposes
3. Species decline due to disease or predation
4. Inadequacy of existing regulatory mechanisms
5. [And] Other natural or man-made factors affecting its continued existence. [7]

"Arguably, plaintiffs meet at least four of the five criteria," Liz continued. "We don't believe the second criterion applies in this instance."

"The government may have a point, Ms. Bay," Chief Justice Taylor began. "You're painting with a broad brush here and concede you have no direct authority for your position."

"Solicitor Paul, does the government believe plaintiffs meet any of the criteria for being listed as endangered under the Act?"

"The government does not, Chief Justice."

"On the contrary," Liz continued, "I believe we've detailed in our briefs how plaintiffs meet the criteria for protection under the Act."

"Deputy marshal, I think we're ready to have plaintiffs brought in," the Chief Justice announced.

"Right away, your honor" the marshal replied, exiting a side door of the courtroom.

The justices appeared to brace themselves. Murmur and rustling swept the courtroom as spectators strained for their best view of the proceedings. The justices had been so strict about

---

[7] <u>Endangered Species Act</u>, 16 U.S.C. § 1533 (1973).

banning animals from the courtroom that spectators were stunned the Court would make any exception. All attention was focused on the courtroom's side door, awaiting the marshal's return.

"Quiet please!" commanded a marshal still inside the courtroom. Outside, attendees drew their animals close in anticipation of seeing the endangered species that would soon be brought inside the courtroom.

After about five minutes the deputy marshal entered the courtroom and stood to the side as six African American males entered the courtroom: four adults, one of them Garrett Granger, and one juvenile carrying an infant. The males approached the plaintiffs' table and remained standing.

VISIONS FROM THE EDGE

A CHRISTMAS WALK TO THE VILLAGE

Tomorrow's the day, Jim Miller mused as he pulled the family transport unit into his garage. *And it'll be Christmas too. Perfect.* Opening the transport door, the voice of his daughter Megan—who was singing inside the house—interrupted his thoughts.

"We're walking, we're walking, we're walking," sang the eight-year-old in a made-up melody, as she danced about the kitchen island where her mother, Fiona, prepared dinner.

"I think you're putting yourself in a trance with that song, Megan, but it's not going to work on me," she laughed. "No one walks to the village around here," she continued. "We're going to ride to the village with our neighbors for hot chocolate and pastries like we always do on Christmas morning, then spend the rest of the day here at home. So no more of this walking nonsense."

"Why doesn't anyone walk, Mom?" Megan asked.

Her ten-year-old brother, Tyler, interrupted before Fiona could formulate a sensitive response.

"But Dad says we're gonna walk tomorrow," he insisted, entering the kitchen after his mother dismissed the idea.

"Walking to the village will be fun. Besides, Dad promised."

"Dad may have promised," Fiona replied, trying her best to sound light-hearted, "but I wasn't a part of that deal, so no deal. I heard the garage door children. Go out and see if your dad needs help bringing in the groceries."

Megan and Tyler flung open the kitchen door that led to the garage just as Jim emerged from the transport unit. Megan ran to grab his hands singing her melody: "We're walking, we're walking, we're walking, Daddy, we're walking to the village tomorrow for Christmas."

"But, Dad," Tyler chimed in, "Mom says we're not walking."

"Of course we are," Jim assured them. "It'll be the family's first walk to the village on Christmas, and I believe it will be our best Christmas ever! C'mon, Megan, help me carry these packages inside. One of the bags has something you and Tyler can put on the tree after dinner. Tyler, plug in the unit for me."

"Presents?" Megan asked, peering into the bags.

"Presents? What presents?" Jim teased.

"It's Christmas, Daddy," said Megan, not taking her father seriously. "I *know* we're getting presents.

Besides, you said there's something me and Tyler can put on the tree."

"Well, would you rather have presents tomorrow or walk to the village?"

"Both!" Tyler replied without hesitation.

"Then both it shall be. Here son, you carry these packages inside. Megan, you and Tyler can open this bag inside the house."

"Hi, sweetheart," said Fiona, giving her husband a brief kiss as he hugged her. "I'm glad you made it back so quickly, given it's Christmas Eve."

"The store wasn't so bad in terms of crowds but the shelves were nearly empty. I was anxious to get back so I could get everything ready for tomorrow."

"We *are* ready, aren't we? What else is left?"

"The Miller family first of course. Our first walk to the village—and on Christmas Day at that!"

"Oh that," said Fiona, momentarily relieved. "The kids have been driving me crazy all day about this supposed walk to the village tomorrow. Why did you tell them we were walking? And how come I didn't know? No one walks anywhere. The neighbors will think we've lost it for sure. Speaking of the neighbors, Ernest and Ruth have invited all of us to ride into the village with their family tomorrow."

Jim's jaw dropped. "But how...?"

"Didn't I tell you? They have a new transport unit that seats eight. It'll be snug but it's much bigger than our four-seater. With her due date for the twins in three months they finally received the government permit for it. I don't think I've ever seen an eight-seater. No one around here has one that I know of."

"That's great for them. Much as I'd like to try it out, I'll forego it for the Miller family excursion on foot. And my dear, we have discussed it."

"But honey, you know as well as I do that no one ever walks to the village. It's too far, especially for the kids, it'll be too cold and—"

"Kids," Jim interrupted, "go check the unit to make sure I didn't forget any packages." With the children out of the kitchen, Jim turned back to his wife. "Those aren't your real concerns, dear."

"You're right," Fiona replied after a brief silence. "We both know it's just too dangerous."

"We have to do this for our children," Jim insisted.

"I don't know what you've told the kids, Jim, but you and I know that no one around here walks— *ever*. It's not likely we'd make it safely to the village on foot. Too much gunfire. And we have to go right past the camps."

"We owe it to our children to at least try," said Jim, hoping to reassure his wife. "We'll all be fine. You'll see. And I promise we'll be safe. Besides we came pretty close to being in the camps ourselves before we moved way out here. The camp dwellers are not all monsters."

"That's true. But the criminal element there worries me. What about our safety, Jim?"

"We'll all be fine, honey. It's time for our children to experience a simple walk in nature."

"It's too dangerous, Jim. The idea of it scares me to death. I can't agree to it."

"Let's agree to disagree for now. I can see this really bothers you. Why don't we continue this later? Is dinner almost done?"

"Just about."

"Nothing in the unit, Dad," Tyler announced as he entered the kitchen with Megan in tow.

"Can we open the package now, Daddy?" she asked.

"You may."

Eyes wide with anticipation, Megan tore through the packages they had carried in earlier until she found one containing a small box.

"For me, Daddy?" she asked, carefully lifting a Christmas ornament from the box.

"For all of us, sweetheart. Tyler, why don't you read it for us?"

"It says, The Miller Family's First Walk to the Village on Christmas. December 25, 2050."

"It's beautiful, Daddy! Can we put it on the tree now?"

"You may. Tyler help her. Then you two cleanup for dinner. It's almost ready."

"That was really thoughtful, Jim," Fiona remarked, after the children left the kitchen. "But you've only made it tougher. I don't want our children walking anywhere. Now they're convinced it's a sure thing."

"Tell you what. Let's continue this discussion after dinner. I'll even do the dishes."

"Nice, but even that won't work."

"Okay then. How about this? I'll need an hour in my workroom after dishes. Then we can put out their toys and I'll make a nice cozy fire just for the two of us."

"You're getting warm. But it still won't work. Why all the mystery about this walk?"

"Consider it my Christmas present to the family."

"Seriously, Jim, I wish you hadn't promised them something so outlandish without discussing it with me first. Well, okay we discussed it, but I didn't think you were serious. I don't want the kids to be disappointed. I can't agree to it. I'd rather they rode in with our neighbors and their children." Turning away from him, she called the kids to dinner.

Jim dropped the subject. No point in arguing on Christmas Eve. But he was undeterred. Once the kids were in bed he'd re-open the discussion in front of the fire with snifters of cognac. That might mellow her mood.

By mid-twenty-first century in some areas of Northern California, it was simply too dangerous outside of a gun-free district to spend any time outside of one's home or bullet-proof transport unit. The Millers lived in a small town in the foothills north of Sacramento. Due to a burgeoning homeless class, which included both employed and unemployed, crime was prevalent from the San Francisco Bay Area all the way to the foothills and beyond, and typically involved guns and other deadly weapons.

The Bay Area's working class and unskilled workers were essentially decimated by the digital age as well as by economic events in the early part of the century. A near depression in the first years of the millennium was followed in later years by political upheaval and instability that affected the nation as a whole. California retained its progressive spirit in the face of it, but still felt the impact.

Hostility to global warming and to global cooperation with other nations resulted in a failure to usher in new industries. After the century's first decade, technology professionals like the Millers' parents rebounded from the economic tsunami, along with their growing families. But they lacked affordable housing. As residential housing prices rose to exorbitant levels, vast numbers of Bay Area residents were forced out of the housing market, even as renters. The wealthiest residents and international investors absorbed most of the available housing in the years that followed.

By 2030, Fiona's parents had tired of moving from bedroom community to bedroom community, far from their Silicon Valley jobs, and moved to Mexico to start a company there. Jim's parents emigrated to Canada.

Jim and Fiona—both substantial earners—had no hope of affordable housing within one hundred fifty miles or so of their jobs, which were also in the Silicon Valley. Even a modest two-bedroom house or apartment, for rent or for sale, was beyond their budget. They briefly tried shared housing with other young families, but found it too chaotic.

As a last resort, the couple searched northeast from the Bay Area toward Sacramento, some 90 miles away. Unable to find affordable housing there, they pushed further north until they located a home in the foothills. With help from their parents they purchased a two-bedroom, one-bath home for nearly $3 million that was more than a century old and needed extensive renovation. Its best feature was a large backyard, which, unfortunately, could not be safely used.

Despite their job stability and relative affluence, the Millers, and others like them, lived as captives in their homes. Materially they lacked little, but lived in close proximity to the homeless camps present in most northern California communities. Some camp residents were still employed, including many of their former colleagues. The vast majority, however, were destitute and desperate.

As robots took over many jobs and technology eliminated others altogether, working class and unskilled workers were forced into itinerant camps due to joblessness, under-employment, and exorbitant housing costs. The camps were not policed or regulated, and law enforcement seldom entered the grounds except when a murder was reported. Camp residents provided whatever shelter they could manage for themselves and their families, from tents to cardboard boxes. The camps were tolerated but not officially sanctioned, and the government provided few resources.

The Millers, and families lucky enough to have housing, hired armed security teams to sleep outside their properties overnight. The security teams were also on hand in the afternoon and early evening when children arrived home from school and their parents home from work. Many tech workers and other professionals worked from home and seldom had to venture out except for business travel and errands. Other professionals like doctors and lawyers, had instituted virtual practices at the turn of the century and no longer maintained offices.

Although the professional classes were materially comfortable and fairly secure inside their homes, they were simply unable to go outside for recreation or relaxation. Gunfire was not uncommon at any hour and spent shell casings were routinely removed from their properties by the private security teams.

Children were never allowed outside to play, as they were likely to encounter gunfire or desperate camp residents looking for food or something to sell. It was against this backdrop that Jim Miller decided to take a stand.

A timid knock on their bedroom door early Christmas morning awakened the couple.

"Enter," said Jim. Megan and Tyler burst through the door and leapt onto their parents' bed, fully dressed to go outside.

"It's still dark outside," said Fiona. "What are you two doing up so early? Have you been downstairs yet?"

"No, Mom," replied Megan. "We're ready for our walk. We just wanted to see if you and Dad were up."

"Not yet as you can see. Go back to bed or go downstairs to see if Santa came. We're not going anywhere before the sun comes up! Merry Christmas, but shut the door." Disappointed, the children slowly climbed off their parents' bed and went downstairs.

"I'm sleepy as hell but now I feel bad," said Jim, after Megan and Tyler reluctantly closed the bedroom door.

"Did you see the look on their faces when they saw us?" Fiona asked. "We've got to get up now. It's Christmas and we may have just ruined it for them. I think you paid them to come in all dressed and ready to go, and then look so pitiful I'd change my mind about the walk. If so, then it worked. I'm officially up. But what will I tell Ernest and Ruth about riding with them?"

"Tell them thank you but we're walking."

Startled by the phone ringing, Fiona wondered who was calling before 6 a.m.

"Merry Christmas. I saw your light and figured you were up," her neighbor Ruth began.

"Merry Christmas, Ruth. The kids just woke us up. I'm glad you called. We want to thank you for inviting us to ride to the village with you this morning but we'd like to take a rain check. It seems we're walking."

"Walking?!" Ruth exclaimed so loudly that Jim could hear her through the phone.

"Walking," Fiona replied in a flat tone. "Jim promised the kids."

"No one walks," said Ruth. "Too dangerous. Hold on. Ernest, you won't believe this. Fiona, Jim and the kids are walking into the village this morning. Yeah, they're walking!"

"What'd he say?" asked Fiona, hopeful Ernest would share her concern.

"He said, "madness" but "Merry Christmas" and that we'll see you there."

Jim quickly dressed while Fiona and Ruth continued to talk, then headed downstairs to start coffee and check on the children. The kids were busy pulling their presents from under the tree and placing them in separate stacks. As excited as they were to open presents, they were more excited to walk. Neither noticed their father watching as they carefully staged their presents for opening later.

After starting coffee Jim entered the garage and accessed the workshop extension he'd built onto it. He immediately powered up the monitor and switched on speakers to contact the night watchmen.

"Merry Christmas, men," he said. "I see you're already having coffee."

"Good morning, sir, and Merry Christmas to you and your family," the head watchman replied.

"Did you have a quiet night?"

"Fairly quiet. Not much gunfire and no prowlers, surprisingly. You're up early, sir."

"The kids got us up. I'm sure you know how that is. And I want you to head home to your families as soon as possible since you'll be returning tonight. We're going to walk into the village this morning."

"Walk? Why on earth, sir? You should have let us know last night. We could have warmed the transport for you."

"Not a problem. We won't need the transport today. We're going to walk. I promised the children. They've never walked anywhere."

"Would you like us to give you cover on the way? We can follow you in our unit as we head home."

"Thanks, but we won't need it. Just signal me an all clear that I can step out. The kids have been dressed since before dawn and Fiona's getting ready. Once I get us all ready to come outside, you can head home for Christmas with your families. Shouldn't take us long."

"Well, we'll pack up our weapons quickly before the kids come outside. Let us know when you're ready to come out with the family and we'll give you the signal. We'll come back for the night watch as usual at 10. Merry Christmas to you and the family, sir, and thanks to you and your wife for the gifts."

"You're welcome, and the same to you and your families."

"Are you sure you don't want us to bring out the transport, sir? We'd give you a lift, but the three of us share a two-person transport as it is. Or, how about we see you at least past the camps between here and the village? We'd feel better."

"Thank you again, but that won't be necessary. You go on home to your families. We'll be fine."

Reluctantly the trio packed their guns, broke down their campsite, and prepared to go home as Jim re-entered the house.

"Is everybody ready?"

"We are! We are!" shouted both children as they ran to their father in the kitchen.

"Where's your mom?"

"She's still upstairs," said Megan. "Is she going with us?"

"Of course she is. Are you both bundled up real good? It's pretty cold," he said, putting his cold hands on their faces.

"Daddy!" Megan laughed, grabbing his hand.

"Fiona—are you almost ready?" Jim called upstairs to his wife.

"I'll be down shortly, honey."

Still can't believe we're doing this, she thought.

"Okay kids, wait here for your mom to come downstairs. I'm going out to the workshop and will be back shortly. Did you have cereal?"

"We're not hungry, Dad," Tyler replied.

While the children waited for their mother to come downstairs, Jim returned to his workshop. The village was not far—roughly two miles from their house. Local tradition gathered townspeople in the village square Christmas mornings to enjoy hot beverages and holiday pastries. The celebration drew residents from miles around but the village was very small. Police would be on hand to organize and direct parking for all the transport units that would jam the square.

Fiona grew increasingly anxious as she waited in the kitchen. She could hear a great deal of commotion coming from the garage, but dared not open the kitchen door to look. The children, on the other hand, could barely contain themselves. Tyler cautiously opened the door to the garage.

"Not yet, son. Close the door," Jim called from the workroom. "We're almost ready." Jim took a final look at the items he'd lined up by the garage door that led outside. Everything was in place. He walked to his monitor and requested an all clear from his watchmen.

"All clear, sir. Merry Christmas."

Once Jim was certain the watchmen's transport unit had backed out of the driveway, he called for Fiona to join him.

"C'mon out, honey, but leave the kids inside for a bit longer while I get you situated."

"We can still ride with the neighbors," Fiona suggested, entering the workroom.

"Much as I'd love to ride in an eight-seater, I'd much rather take a walk with my family. A Christmas morning walk," Jim said, suddenly more earnest than teasing. He stopped his preparations and turned to his wife, putting his hands on her shoulders and turning her toward him. "Honey. Our children have never gone for a walk outside. We haven't walked outside since they were born."

"But Jim, it's just too dangerous," Fiona replied, fear taking over. "We're not in a gun-free district, you know. Only God knows if we'll ever win *that* lottery. Then we could be outside as much as we wanted. Even enjoy our huge backyard."

"Who knows? It could be tomorrow. Or never. I'm tired of waiting. Waiting just to be able to walk down the damn street. Breathe fresh air. Feel the sun on my body. Let the children experience and enjoy nature."

"Oh no!" Fiona exclaimed. "That reminds me—I didn't put sun block on the kids."

"Leave it, honey. For once I want them to experience a walk in fresh air and sunshine. I want them to absorb every ray! All they've known until now is high dose vitamin D tablets and sun lamps year-round."

"But where are the watchmen? You didn't let them go already did you?"

"Of course I did, but not before they gave me an all clear. It's Christmas for them too. I wanted them to get home to their families."

"But they could have seen us safely past the camps and to the village."

"They offered, but no need, dear. We'll all be fine. Come. I'll get you set up first."

"Jim, what the...?"

Jim directed his wife to one of four Lucite-like forms, one of which matched her height. Each form resembled a jumpsuit with a slender opening along the side from head to toe, which Jim gently nudged Fiona through.

"It's your own personal walkabout honey. Walking suit is probably a better name for it. It has its own force field, which will keep anyone away from you and is bullet-proof like the transports. Look here—you even have a sun roof."

"Where on earth did you get these, Jim?"

"I made them."

"No way!"

"It's true, I made them."

"No, Jim. I mean there's *no way* me and the kids are going anywhere in these things. Suits."

"Courage, dear. I won't let anything happen to you or the kids. I'll also be armed as usual."

"Oh, and that's supposed to make me feel better?"

"Go on, step fully inside and take a look at the controls. I'll explain them when I get the kids set up."

He called into the house. "Okay, kids, c'mon out."

Tyler and Megan dashed from the kitchen, through the garage into the workroom, eyes wide when they saw their mom and the gear waiting for them.

"What's this, Dad?" Tyler asked.

"What do we do, Daddy?" Megan chimed in.

"These are your very own walking suits, kids. Step inside and I'll explain everything."

"They look so funny, Daddy. Is this what we're walking in?"

"Right you are, daughter. Just step through the opening there."

"These are so cool, Dad," said Tyler. "Where'd you get them?"

"Made 'em myself, son," Jim replied, beaming.

"You mean you invented these, Dad?"

"I did, Tyler. For you and Megan. I wanted you to be able to walk outside. Let me show you how it works.

"From a distance it looks like hard plastic," Jim explained, "but it's actually a more flexible material—a Jim Miller secret—and it will move with you. Each of you has a small sunroof—the button right there opens and closes it. You have heat and cold air. That's controlled here. We also have intercom. We all have individual controls inside our suits and I have the master controls for everyone.

"Now," Jim continued, "safety is important on our walk, just like it always is when we're out together. When we pass the camps, people there may be curious and come out to look. That's okay. But if they get too close—say from here to the wall over there—you can turn on your force field by pressing here. That will keep anyone from getting too close to us. What does the big red button say, Megan?"

"Go away."

"That's right, sweetheart. And if you press the red button that's exactly what they'll do. Don't worry about it today, though. Every button that's in your suits is also in mine and I can press that button for you if needed."

"Jim..." Fiona began, looking directly at her husband while trying to disguise the alarm in her voice.

"Any questions, now's the time to ask," Jim replied, trying to acknowledge Fiona's concern without alarming the kids. "Okay then. Let's head out!"

The family left the workroom and exited the house from the garage door on the side of the house. As they walked down the driveway to the street, a stream of transport units snaked slowly in front of their house toward the village. Once the Millers reached the sidewalk and walked parallel to the transports, traffic nearly stopped as drivers and their passengers strained to catch a glimpse of the family.

Jim was thrilled to watch his children walk—awkwardly at first—then run and play along the street in their suits, waving to the children and adults who waved back at them. Even Fiona's fears lessened as she watched her children playing in the sunshine.

"All right children, we're approaching the camps up ahead there, so come back and remain close to Mommy and Daddy," Jim cautioned. "Just remember, we're right here and won't let anything happen to you. I'm going to activate one big force field for us."

"I'm not worried, Dad," said Tyler.

"Neither am I, Daddy," said Megan. "This is the best Christmas ever!"

Jim was warmed by his children's courage, but still concerned about Fiona's apprehension.

As they approached the camps, Megan and Tyler ran back to walk between their parents. As the Millers drew close to the first one, camp sentries immediately stood and formed a protective wall around the entrance. Each sentry was armed with a shotgun, but kept it at his or her side with the barrel pointed to the sky. Many of the camp dwellers strained to get a glimpse of the Millers through the sentries' blockade. Fiona refused to look toward the camp, but Megan and Tyler appeared drawn to something there, and stared as they walked past.

Jim quietly suggested to the children via intercom that they not stare. Much to Fiona's relief, the family passed the one-mile site on its outermost rim without incident. Jim was proud of his children's courage and, once they were clear of the area, allowed them to once again run and play as they continued toward the village.

At the café, the Millers claimed a table big enough to accommodate themselves and their neighbors. Everyone stared as the family entered in their suits. Their curiosity was obvious, but no one approached them right away. The family quickly shed the suits and settled at the table. Jim placed the walking suits in a hallway off the main dining area that led to the kitchen and a rear service door.

Just then Ernest and Ruth entered the café with their children and joined them, grateful the Millers had found a table. Too excited to stay seated, the children ran off to greet their friends in the café.

"Your eight-seater looks sharp, Ernest," said Jim. "Saw you on our way in."

"Saw you, too. What on earth? Can't believe you walked to the village. Glad you made it safely, but have you lost your mind? What were those things anyway?"

"Walkabouts or walking suits. We—okay, *I* wanted the children to experience a simple walk outside. They can do almost anything indoors, but I wanted them to feel sun and fresh air on their faces and see trees and shrubs up close."

"Well, I'd like my kids to experience a walk, but it's just too dangerous. Did you have any trouble passing the camps?"

"No. It was a bit tense though, as you don't know what to expect. I thought the kids would be anxious passing them, but they seemed more curious than anything else. They both just stared and I had to warn Tyler not to stare or point. But after we passed the camps, they took off running and playing again. And Fiona was a trouper. I didn't expect trouble, but we were prepared. The suits are bulletproof and have a force field surround. Plus, who isn't armed?"

"You know it."

"I've been working on them for two years. Primitive, but it's the best I could do in my garage and workroom. I'm already thinking improvements. Would you like a demonstration?"

"Sure, how about tomorrow? In your driveway."

"That'll work. I'm also working on something similar for the kids in our backyard—a domed play area. Fiona teases that I'm building another house."

"Most of our lots have small houses, but backyards big enough to do that," Ernest added.

Concerned about Fiona, Ruth turned to her. "You look a little worse for wear my friend, but you made it."

"I'm not surprised the journey shows on my face. I feel even worse than that, but I'm grateful the children made it. I have to admit—the look on their faces as they ran and played was priceless. Such pure joy and abandonment. It's what we'd all like for our children."

"You keep working on it, Jim," Ruth replied. "Maybe by the time our twins are walking we'll be able to join you."

"Glad to see you're holding up, Fiona," Ernest added.

"You're still welcome to ride home with us in the transport."

"Let's just say I could probably use something stronger than coffee right now, but I'll leave it at that. Thank you for the offer though. The kids really enjoyed the walk here. I think the people in the camps were so surprised to see us walking that they just stared, but let us be. God, they looked so forlorn. Christmas morning and you just know most of them are cold and numb from camping out night after night. I'm sure they're hungry, too. And probably little, if anything, for the kids in the way of Christmas gifts."

"Ernest, you ever stop to think that we could have been in those camps?" Jim asked. "That there are people there who once had homes? And good jobs? I know we're supposed to see them as dangerous—less than human even—but I can certainly identify with some of them."

"I know. We used to work with a lot of them."

"Ah, here come our pastries and hot chocolate," Fiona announced. Looking around the café, she saw their children at a nearby table. "Okay kids, our food is here."

"Merry Christmas, everyone!" Fiona stated with as much cheerfulness as she could muster when the children returned to the table. "And look, it's starting to snow."

For the next couple of hours, Christmas festivities overshadowed any concerns Fiona may have had about returning home on foot.

"Merry Christmas! How are you folks doing today?" café owner Ned Parsons called out as he approached their table.

"We're all fine, Ned," Jim replied. "The same to you."

"I haven't had a chance to ask you about the contraptions you put back in my hallway there. Been too busy as you can see. But I'm gonna have

87

to hear all about it later. We've just put in our last batch of pastries for the day. Will you be wanting anything else this morning? Or to take home? Megan and Tyler, how many of the Christmas cookies have you had so far? Last year you packed 'em in."

"Four for me," Tyler said proudly.

"Two for me," Megan added.

"Well, we've got a fresh batch coming out in a couple of minutes. Wanna come back and pack up a few more to take home?"

"Can we, Mom?" Megan asked.

"Sure, but not too many."

"We should be heading back soon, Jim. There's already a light dusting of snow on the ground and it's still coming down."

"We've still got room in the transport," Ernest offered again.

"Jim, maybe we should."

"Honey, we'll be fine. Besides we can't deprive our children of their first snowball fight."

"Well, I'll go get them while you get our gear."

"C'mon, dear," Ernest said to Ruth. "Let's bundle our squad and head out."

"Jim! Come quick! The kids are gone!" Fiona cried out as she ran from the kitchen into the café dining room.

"What? Gone? Gone where?"

"They're not in the kitchen. They're gone, Jim! My babies are gone!"

"Ned, weren't you in the kitchen with the kids?" Jim asked, trying not to appear as frantic as he felt. "Where are they?"

Ned, shock apparent on his face, was at a loss to explain.

"Yes. Yes, Jim. They were boxing up the cookies. I left the kitchen to bring out a few takeout orders. The ovens were all off in there so I thought it would be okay."

"Someone call the police," Fiona demanded, her panic rising. "Jim, check our gear. Is theirs still back there?" Jim ran to the alcove where he'd stored their walking suits and found all four suits still there.

"Everything's still there!" he shouted, running back to the dining room.

"My babies, Jim! Where are they? They're out there in the cold somewhere or someone took them! You've got to find our babies!"

Customers still at the café immediately sprang into action and ran outside with the couple to look for the children. The police response was immediate as a few off duty officers were already on hand to direct traffic. One of the officers ran up to them.

"I see some tiny shoe prints in the snow across the street headed that way, away from the square."

"That's towards our house," Jim began.

"It's also towards the camps, Jim!" Fiona added.

"C'mon, you two," Ernest commanded. "You're definitely riding with us this time. Let's go!"

One patrol car, following the small footprints, raced toward the camps with Ernest's family and the Millers close behind. As everyone feared, the shoe prints stopped in front of one of the camps. Armed camp sentries blocked the entrance, as the lone police officer approached with gun drawn. Jim bounded from Ernest's transport unit and approached the sentries.

"My children are in there and I've come to get them. I don't want anyone to get hurt. We're all armed to kill. I just want my children."

The lead sentry—keeping his eye on the officer—addressed his team of guards before responding to Jim.

"The officer here will have backup soon. Go out and block the road."

"Not a good idea," the officer replied. "You're right. I'll have backup soon."

"Until then, you're outnumbered," the sentry replied.

"I don't want any trouble," Jim repeated. "I just want my children. Give them up and I won't press charges."

"We don't have your kids," the lead sentry replied. "Only our own."

"I know our kids are in there," Fiona stepped forward, suddenly emboldened. "Megan, Tyler, are you in there? Don't be afraid. We've come to get you. Megan, Tyler, answer me!"

"We're in here, Mommy," Megan called out in a quiet voice.

"Let us in or it's on," Jim demanded, putting his hand on his gun. The other sentries immediately raised their weapons.

"All right. Everyone stand down!" the lead sentry commanded his team. "Make way and let these two in."

"Four," Ernest interrupted. "We're going in too," he added, nodding at his wife.

The officer kept his gun pointed at the lead sentry, certain the backup police officers were in a standoff with the other sentries down the road.

The sentries guarding the camp cleared a small entryway for the Millers and their neighbors. Behind them, the camp dwellers moved aside to reveal Tyler and Megan walking further into the campsite, carrying a large metal urn between them and stacks of tied boxes in their free hand.

"What the...?" Jim began. "Megan, Tyler, are you okay?"

As Jim and Fiona rushed to embrace their children, Megan and Tyler quickly dropped the urn and boxes.

"What are you doing here?" Fiona asked.

"Don't be mad, Mom and Dad," Tyler began. "We had to come here. On the way to the village we saw some of the kids we used to go to school with. And a lot of other kids. They all looked so cold and hungry. And it's Christmas. We wanted them to have a little of what we had earlier.

"So when Mr. Parsons left the kitchen, Megan and I tied up as many boxes of cookies and pastries as we could carry with one hand and picked up the urn of hot chocolate Mr. Parsons had made for another family. We didn't want anyone to see us so we took off out the back door. Is Mr. Parsons mad?"

"I'm sure he's just concerned about you both, like we all were," a relieved Fiona responded. "You can apologize to him later and come up with a plan to pay him back."

"We're okay, Mom," said Tyler. "They even brought us blankets to put on. They're just cold and hungry and sad because it's Christmas."

"That's why we wanted to keep 'em," said the lead sentry, now smiling. "Your kids brought something no one here dared expect—Christmas. You'll always have safe passage here—with or without those suits."

"C'mon then, children," said Fiona. "Let's finish what you started. Merry Christmas, everyone," she added, opening the boxes of pastries and setting them on a makeshift table the camp dwellers quickly cleared.

Jim and Ernest hoisted the urn of hot chocolate onto the table and took turns filling whatever cup or dish the camp dwellers presented. After the distribution, the Millers sent their children and two of the walking suits home with Ernest and Ruth, despite the children's protests, and walked the rest of the way together.

"I feel so ashamed, Jim. Where did our children get their courage? Certainly not from me. I never knew Megan was so fierce and Tyler so brave. I've only fed them fear."

"You stepped up when it counted back there. I was proud of you."

"I can't believe how many people we recognized in that camp, Jim. They all have young children like ours."

"Guess that's why the children slowed down on the way to the village. They recognized old friends."

"You know that domed playground in the backyard you're working on that I call a house?"

"You read my mind. I'm sure we can get some of our neighbors on board to do the same."

"Ironic about our kids isn't it, Jim?"

"How so, dear?"

"Looks like today's walk was good for their bodies and everyone's spirits."

VISIONS FROM THE EDGE

THE SOLITARY READER

Dalton's relaxed demeanor as he sat reading in his favorite chair belied the predicament he was in. Two books—the one he was reading and the one that lay on the floor—would decide his fate. Notwithstanding his dilemma, he continued to read with laser focus.

"Two *more* books?" his exasperated wife Nora shouted from outside his workroom door earlier that evening. Through a peephole in the door she observed a teetering stack of books behind his chair that nearly reached the ceiling. The stack had been half that size earlier in the day.

"That's what you've been promising all weekend, you asshole. You would read two more books, and then spend time with me. Well that was God knows how many books ago and you're still reading. Enough!

"Your books breed like rabbits," she snorted in disgust as she entered the room. "And they're illegal for God's sake. Look at all the additional books you've read since this morning! It's a wonder I haven't turned you in by now. Don't think I'm going to pick up all of those damn books when they fall. I told you last week that if you brought any more of those books into the house this weekend, they would be your last. Obviously you didn't believe me, you bastard. But I'm gonna make a believer out of you today. Do you hear me, asshole? Say something!"

Dalton heard her. He always did. She knew he didn't like to be disturbed while reading. But she ignored his desire for privacy and he ignored her. They had danced this dance for years and both were weary of it but unwilling to stop.

"I know you hear me, asshole."

"Of course, dear. I always do," Dalton replied, knowing he *must* say something at this point. He did not relish her new pejorative names for him or even remember the last time Nora had used his name or any term of endearment. To mention it now, however, would only add fuel to the fire. "I guess I got carried away. I'll be done soon. Then we can go for a walk and get ice cream."

"A walk? Ice cream? Are you kidding me? We won't be doing anything together. This is it. I told you. We're done. You're done. Tell you what, asshole. I'm locking you in. If you can get those last two books on top of that shaky stack without toppling your precious tower, I'll unlock the door in the morning. If even one of your blessed books falls from that stack, I'm going to set this house on fire with you and all your precious books in it!"

"They won't fall, dear," Dalton reassured with maddening calm. "Everything's going to be fine. The stack will hold. No mess to clean up. Then I promise. I'll come out and we'll have a long talk. I know I've been promising that for a long time. This time I'll make good. Just these last two."

Reading came early for Dalton. One day while still a toddler he picked up his father's newspaper and began reading. His astounded parents never made a big production of it. They simply indulged his passion for reading to the exclusion of typical childhood activities like sports, and were not particularly concerned that he had few friends.

Nothing could separate Dalton from his beloved books. Not the law, which banned all paper books on January 1, 2040—a day he'd never forget but one he refused to acknowledge. Not even his ranting wife, who threw down the gauntlet time and time again. Granted, she'd never threatened to put match to house and book before. However, Dalton took that as the depth of her frustration, not deadly intent. There was no question he loved her. Problem for them was that he could not love her in the way she needed. She needed his attention. He needed to read. From paper books. Not digital books or even the 3D books available online.

Paper books had fallen victim to the digital age and green movement. Nora hadn't minded and quickly fell in line. However, Dalton resisted the ban along with countless other book lovers, who maintained a thriving underground trade in the contraband. Just when Nora was certain she had rooted out and destroyed her husband's stash of books, a fresh crop appeared.

The fact that he and Nora once enjoyed reading together was now hard to believe. On their first date, they sat by the fire after dinner and read to each other. He fell in love with her that night, envisioning weekends together at the library, scouring shops for rare books and slowly building a well-stocked library at home.

They lived Dalton's dream the first two years of married life. Neither of them desired children. But over time, Nora grew restless then jealous, as Dalton grew more content with reading to the exclusion of everything else. The ensuing guerilla warfare skirmishes over Dalton's incessant reading, and refusal to join the digital reading world, had pocked their marriage ever since.

When Nora discovered that Dalton had secreted away some 70 books in his workroom since last week's warning, something in her gave way. She had long ago given up on her other interests, the running of her home, and life in general. And even though she once loved to read, Nora had grown so resentful of Dalton's incessant reading that she refused to read to spite him. Dalton barely took note of his wife's deterioration: her unkempt appearance, frayed nightgown that also served as day wear, or the overall slovenly appearance of their once well-ordered home.

He briefly considered that his wife's threat could be problematic, but quickly resumed his reading. He wasn't excessively worried. Nora was confident she knew every hiding place for Dalton's books. He knew better. To divert her relentless searching this time, he put his latest cache of books on full view. He had not stacked the massive tower of books behind his chair by hand, although it appeared that way to Nora. Instead he had rigged a makeshift pulley from tools in his workroom—courtesy of a book he'd read years ago.

Dalton could not bear to look at piles of books while reading—one of his idiosyncrasies. He did not like the distraction. He preferred building a tower of books behind his well-worn reading chair that he could admire once he was done reading for the day. He was happiest when the stack of completed books reached the ceiling. He was certain he could hoist the last two books for today atop the stack without incident. Nora would have no reason to torch him, the house, or his beloved books.

Outside the workroom, Nora raged all over the house, breaking dishes, furniture, and anything in her path until she wore herself out and fell asleep. Dalton finished the last book an hour before the raging ended and puttered around the workroom to distract himself from growing hunger. He could have opened the door from the inside but preferred the solitude.

It was nearly daylight when Dalton awakened to Nora's footsteps approaching his workroom.

"Well, asshole, did you give up? There's no way you could have stacked those books to the ceiling without the stack falling. Are you ready to burn in hell, because I've got my torches ready!" Dalton slowly stood up from the chair as he heard Nora reach the door.

"Good morning, dear," Dalton replied with resignation, speaking to his wife through the door. "Do you think I could get a cup of coffee? Better yet, why don't you just come in and have coffee with me? If you're up to it, we can talk now. All day if you want."

"I'm not making coffee, asshole. You'll get your next cup in hell," Nora vowed, again putting her eye to the peephole in the door. Stunned by what she saw, she took the key from her pocket and unlocked the door.

"What? There's no way those books didn't fall. It's impossible!"

"Tell you what, dear," Dalton replied calmly. "Why don't you sit down here and *I'll* make us both some coffee. Then we can sit out on the patio and drink it. Looks like a nice morning."

"I don't want any coffee, asshole. I want to know how you got those books stacked like that without one of them bringing the whole stack down."

"I'll explain it over coffee, sweetheart," Dalton replied quietly, as he exited the workroom for the kitchen.

Early as it was, Nora's resumed ranting pierced the quiet of a promising morning. Once in the hallway, Dalton glanced back at his newly irate wife with affection and gently closed the door. It was only when she heard the key lock the door that Nora smelled the smoke.

DUMB KIDS LIVE THERE

"All right everyone, listen up," Captain Dodd called out above the noisy din of the precinct briefing room. "Before I do the briefing this morning, I want to get my DK Patrol Team out of here and on the street."

"No point in keeping us in mystery, Captain," said Officer Taylor. "You know how much we all love DK patrol. Who are the lucky ones today?"

"Glad you asked, Taylor," Captain Dodd replied. "You are. And since you showed so much interest by raising the question, I'm putting you in charge of the team today. Officers Bretton and Thompson will assist. Have a nice day gentlemen. You're outta here!"

Officer Taylor's colleagues laughed, some of them patting him on the back, relieved they would not have the patrol today. Everyone hated the assignment.

"My kids go to school," Officer Taylor muttered as he grabbed his equipment. "I don't understand these parents who can't get their kids to go. Besides, it's the law."

"Well, I don't know," Officer Bretton argued. "What are the parents to do? They can't force them."

"The hell!" Officer Thompson replied. "Even when it means the parents' hard-earned paychecks will be docked as a result?"

"Figure it out in the field," Captain Dodd interrupted. "I gotta briefing here I need to finish." Shaking his head, Officer Taylor left the room with his team.

"Hope you're wearing the latest sneakers today," Captain Dodd called out to the departing team. "You're gonna need 'em."

The officers' laughter at Dodd's remark further irritated Taylor as he left the police briefing room. After all of his training to prepare for much tougher challenges, today he was assigned to look for, chase, and detain kids who did not want to go to school. The "dumb kids" or "DK" patrol as they affectionately called it.

School attendance seven days a week was mandatory in the San Francisco Bay area in the latter part of the twenty-first century, and had been for many years. Children were no longer able to drop out of school. Nor were they able to apply for any job without at least a high school diploma. General Education Diplomas were no longer conferred.

Non-attendance brought escalating penalties for the first three instances up to and including detention for thirty days in the local juvenile

104

facility. In addition, parents were ordered jailed or fined after the third incidence of their child's non-attendance.

School age youth unaccompanied by adults were not allowed on city streets during school hours, and, if spotted alone on the streets at those times, were subject to detention by police. Upon the first instance of non-attendance, parents were notified and, after a written warning, allowed to pick up their child from the detention center. After a second incident, the child was jailed overnight and parents were notified of their child's court hearing the next day, at which time the court set conditions for the child's release. After a third offense, the child was ordered held for one month in the juvenile detention center.

If the non-attendance continued, the next stop was a one-year sentence to the Alcatraz Island Juvenile Remediation Center, originally a lighthouse, then a Bay Area adult prison and later, a popular tourist attraction.

Parents were held strictly liable for their child's non-attendance at school. If the youth was sent to Alcatraz, the parents' wages would be garnished monthly for the child's support, unless they were able to pay outright. The children were supposed to attend school on the island but this regulation was not monitored or strictly enforced.

California school children, like school age children around the U.S., had fallen woefully behind their counterparts in other countries in so-called STEM[8] subjects starting at the end of the twentieth century. Not only had America suffered in its ability to lead innovation and advancements in important areas, the increasing divide between the highly skilled tech workers in the Silicon Valley and non-tech workers in the Bay Area had brought the area to near social and economic chaos. This was no more evident than in the struggle to find housing, which became increasingly unaffordable even for many of the affluent, especially once the area recovered from the Great Recession at the turn of the century.

Coupled with the state's own financial woes as a result of the recession, money for education was severely cut and teacher pay was insufficient for retention. As a result the state experienced a rising school dropout rate and teacher shortage it was unable to slow or reverse.

Decades earlier, after political policy slowly redirected funds for public education to private schools and voucher academies, the federal government abdicated responsibility for existing national education standards in favor of the states' right to set their own agendas. California families unable to afford private schools were forced to send their children to public schools, which were poorly resourced and nearly abandoned.

---

[8] Science, Technology, Engineering, Math

Young adults, many of whom were the product of these schools and lacked a solid high school education or trade skills, found it difficult to gain a toehold in society. Even those with higher education and technical training often bemoaned the lack of good jobs. Consequently, many young people in the area's middle and high schools saw no point in attending school at all. Despite the San Francisco area's supply of technical jobs, the rapid pace of technological change required increasingly sophisticated skill sets that many simply did not have.

For years, Bay Area companies, especially those in Silicon Valley, recruited engineers, scientists, and other technical professionals from other nations to keep up with demand and, according to some views, pay lower wages. While the aggressive overseas recruiting helped, it simply could not keep pace with demand.

Faced with the growing need for a highly skilled workforce in the region, the Bay Area's tech giants implemented public-private partnerships with the area's public school systems in an effort to transform education and provide skilled candidates for their companies. Industry leaders also lobbied the California legislature to make high school graduation mandatory.

As a result, public schools in the region saw infusions of private capital they had previously only dreamed of. All children were now thoroughly evaluated upon entering elementary school for educational aptitude, learning disorders, emotional fitness, and mental health issues. Even children with learning and cognitive disabilities were evaluated and provided with targeted education and skills training. The goal was to provide all children with whatever they needed in order to succeed and be productive members of the community.

"We just got a call, Taylor," Officer Bretton reported as the team patrolled the streets near one of the local middle schools. "Team of kids seen tagging over on Dover and Ridge."

"Tell 'em to have a couple of squad cars meet us there," Officer Taylor replied. "We're only a block away."

As the officers rounded the corner they observed four young people spray painting what appeared to be a house undergoing renovation. The teens were so busy they did not observe the DK team approaching on foot and the squad cars quietly parking across the street. The officers had time to spread out and block any escape route their soon-to-be captives might try.

"Okay, kids. Drop the paints and turn around with your hands up," commanded Officer Taylor. Too startled to run, two youths dropped their paint cans and slowly turned to face the officers. The other two immediately bolted but stopped as soon as they saw they were surrounded.

108

"Well, look who we have here," said Taylor as he searched, then handcuffed one of the youths. "My favorite crew! We've taken all of you into custody before so you know the drill. At least we didn't have to chase you over field and stream today. Mr. James, I believe this is a fourth strike for you."

"It's a fourth for Mr. Willard and Mr. Roberts too; third time for the other one," said Bretton.

Oliver James, a fifteen-and-a-half-year-old serial tagger well known to officers, remained silent.

"You know where you're headed this time, don't you, Mr. James?" Taylor asked.

"I don't wanna go there! Dumb kids live there and I hear some of 'em never get out."

"Well, you'll soon see whether that's true or not. I told you the last time there'd be a bed waiting for you at Alcatraz if you didn't go to school. You and your crew act dumb as hell, but I'm sure there's some kinda talent here. Why aren't you in the art programs at school? I told you they have tagging competitions there for big prizes."

"Man, I ain't got no time for those squares."

"Right. Obviously, you've got time to spend a year in Alcatraz cuz that's probably where you're headed. We got 'em all team? Okay then. Into the squad cars boys. We're headed to juvy. We'll notify your parents about your court hearing tomorrow."

"My parents probably won't show this time," said one of the youths.

"They have to or they get an automatic week in jail," Taylor replied.

The youths' court hearing the next morning was brief. All of their parents and the parents of six other children detained the previous day were present, many of them tearful, some angry they missed work. Of the ten, six were second-timers and were released to their parents under strict conditions. Oliver and his tagging crew were the last ones addressed by the judge.

"Good morning, gentlemen," she began.

"Good morning," two of the less sullen youths mumbled in response.

"You all entered your pleas earlier this morning so I'll proceed to sentencing. What I'm about to do in your case is at odds with our goals for you in this community but I must follow the law. Mr. Owens, I'm informed this is your third strike. You are sentenced to serve thirty days in the juvenile detention center here. As for the remaining three, Mr. James, Mr. Roberts, and Mr. Willard, each of you is hereby sentenced to one year at the Alcatraz Island Youth Remediation Center."

"Dumb kids live there and I don't wanna go!" Oliver blurted out. "I need to be home with my family and go to school here."

"The truth is, Mr. James," the judge continued, "you were absolutely willing to go Alcatraz and join all the other "dumb kids"—as you call them—who currently live there. You've had three chances to

110

attend school and remain in the community with your family and you blew all three. The law says I must send you away for a year. Do I want to send you? No. I believe you're all too young to appreciate what I'm about to tell you but I'm required to do so. I hope you'll listen well."

"I ain't got time for this crap," Oliver muttered.

"Close your ears if you like, but for the next few minutes you'll also need to close your mouth," the judge replied.

"In fact, we've tried to reinforce this information from the first day you attended school. Each of you is so important to our community, to this nation. I'm sure that's hard for you to grasp at fourteen and fifteen. Especially when you're about to be locked up. But it boils down to this: there will be no place for you in this or any other community in our state—in our country for that matter—unless you get an excellent education. Not just a good education but an excellent education. And that's now available to each of you and to every child in this state."

Blah, blah, blah, Oliver thought.

"By law you must at least achieve a high school diploma in order to work or go on to college. And once you get your diploma you're going to have to compete for a job as though you were competing for an Olympic team. You won't be just competing against each other but against your peers from all over the world. Peers who don't have a problem

111

going to school. Peers with few opportunities in their own countries who are working hard to gain entry here and compete against you.

"If you don't achieve the minimum requirement of a high school diploma, a more enterprising youth or a young person from another country may very well win the job you want, as well as your place in this community. And as your parents well know, unless you have a job you cannot qualify for housing in the Bay Area. Without at least a high school diploma, you will have no job and no money for even shared housing. What will you do then? At least one year of adult prison. After that, possible banishment to one of the lawless zones.

"These rules are relatively new for all of us," the judge continued. "As recently as 2020 or so, young people could drop out of school and work two or three low-wage jobs to get by. But those days are over. Many of those jobs are now performed by robots or have been eliminated altogether. The jobs that are left require a high level of skill, education, and training."

"But I hear some kids never get out of Alcatraz," Oliver interrupted.

"In rare cases that's true for some young people until they reach 18. After that they go to prison for one year if they haven't earned a diploma. But that does not have to be your fate."

"I just can't do school," Oliver insisted.

"Oh, you can. Your trouble is that you won't—big difference. As a matter of fact, I'm puzzled that the three of you are even here again. You are free to choose what you want to learn in our community schools and will be provided all the resources needed to succeed. The fact that you all like to tag suggests you have artistic ability. Have you tried that path?"

"That shit's for squares," Oliver mumbled under his breath.

"What's that?"

"School is for squares," Oliver declared, looking directly at the judge.

"Your answer, Mr. James, suggests you've not attended school long enough to find out what's available there. Maybe *that's* "square" to use your word. Any high school graduate who wants to attend college may do so at no cost. If you prefer to learn a skill or trade, you are eligible to apply for an apprenticeship during your last year of high school. If you want to be your own boss you can apply for the entrepreneurship program in high school. That's the most popular program in the Bay Area."

"That's all we ever hear: stem, stem, stem. Some of us just can't do that stuff."

"STEM courses are favored of course, but music and the arts are also encouraged. Why? It makes us well rounded. Moreover, we now have the highest standard of living ever in this region-in the country for that matter-and the goal is to enjoy an even higher standard of living in the years to come. That's where you come in. The law says you must contribute to the community to the best of your ability in order to live here, whether it's in the arts, science, technology, business, or skilled trades. Your only job now is to be a good citizen and get an education. By the way, the military won't even look at you until you have at least two years of college under your belt."

"I'm willing to attend school tomorrow, ma'am," said one of the youths. "Can't you just give me one more chance and send me home today?"

"Well, in your case Mr. Roberts, we've tried that three times and you still failed to attend school. Now I have to do my job and send you away for a while. One year. And I tell you all, you'll have to work harder than ever to get an education at Alcatraz. You'll better understand what I mean when you get there. Good luck, gentlemen.

"As for the parents of the three youths going to Alcatraz, I sentence each of you to one week in county jail. However, because my information is that you made reasonable efforts to comply with school attendance laws, I will stay that sentence for now. If upon your child's release he has an additional finding of non-attendance, I will impose the one-week jail term stayed here today as well as a possible fine. You are hereby assessed for your child's room and board at Alcatraz. You may pay in full or make payment arrangements before you leave here today. Otherwise your paychecks and/or business accounts will be garnished. Court is adjourned."

The judge rose from the bench, briefly surveying the tearful parents and shocked youths she'd just sentenced. She understood both sides all too well. She and her husband had three teenagers, one of whom had little use for school. But for the grace of God thus far, she sat on the bench and not in the courtroom with the other parents. She could join them yet.

Oliver had struggled with behavioral issues at home and in school since age five. He was diagnosed with ADHD[9] and, more recently, with ODD[10], but his parents had refused medications suggested for him. They also failed to take advantage of non-medication interventions that were available and did not make time to form a partnership with school staff to address his needs.

Schools were willing to work with Oliver, but his parents, having no control over their son by age 10, simply threw up their hands and abdicated. Abandoned, Oliver resolved to avoid any educational path and instead, pursue his penchant for tagging whenever and wherever he could. This time that penchant would deposit him in Alcatraz. As he was led out of the courtroom a still belligerent Oliver

---

[9] Attention Deficit Hyperactivity Disorder
[10] Oppositional Defiance Disorder

vowed to serve his time and go right back to tagging. And that was his mindset as he and his crew arrived at Alcatraz.

"Well if it ain't the little bitches from south of Market," called out Juan, one of the Alcatraz residents, as Oliver and the others arrived in the main hall after orientation. The sixteen-year-old Juan was ten months into his year-long sentence. "I've seen your work in my hood you little bitches and it ain't shit. Good thing five-0 got you before we did because we don't like people taggin' on our turf."

"Juan, that's not how we welcome," a staff officer intervened. "Take a seat. Now!"

Oliver was prepared to confront the youth, but staff intervention stopped him for now. However, Oliver and his crew knew they would have to respond to Juan's disrespect eventually if they were going to survive.

"All right," the staff officer began. "Everyone listen up. School will start in fifteen minutes at 8:30 sharp. I want to see a butt in every seat and I don't want to hear a peep out of anyone unless you're asked to speak. We'll have a thirty-minute break for lunch at 12:30, after which you'll have a fifteen-minute break to use the john. After that you will have sports outside for forty-five minutes. School resumes at 2:30 until 5:30. Dinner from 5:45 to 6:15. Afterward, those of you due to have phone or video chat time with your family will have ten minutes each. The rest of you have indoor recreation and/or free time. Lights out at 8:30 p.m., 9:00 for those with sufficient points. Okay. Let's lineup for school."

Stupid rules, Oliver thought as he lined up with the others. The very reason he refused to attend school. All of the stupid rules. He would comply enough to do his time here and get out. Hopefully, Juan's payback would be under the radar and not cost him additional time. On the other hand, being called out by Juan in front of the others really pissed him off. Payback might be worth extra time, he reasoned, as he took a seat and waited for class to begin.

When it did, all hell broke loose and Oliver was jolted from his thoughts of revenge on Juan by the scene before him. This was unlike any classroom he'd ever been in.

Here at Alcatraz, like in his old classrooms, the coursework was mostly online via computer screens built into the desk. However, many of the screens in this classroom were smashed and some desks had no computer screens at all. Fights broke out the minute class began. Anything not tied down or secured was subject to being thrown at someone or launched across the room just for the hell of it. Some students lucky enough to have working computers at their desks tried to complete their work notwithstanding the noise and chaos. Others just put their heads down on the desks. Oliver

117

learned during his orientation that staff would mace the most violent fighters rather than intervene, which would effectively end class for everyone.

Classrooms at his old school were so quiet they put him to sleep almost from the moment he sat down. Once the teachers there explained the day's lessons, he pretty much tuned out or dozed off until the end-of-class bell rang. Although his teachers and their assistants offered him any help he might need, Oliver refused it all. He endured school so he and his crew could tag on the way home. Sometimes they'd sneak out at night to tag. Nothing else mattered to Oliver. He was unable to stop and didn't want to, even if he could. His squad wound up at Alcatraz this time because they brazenly tagged during school hours, even though they knew they would be subject to arrest and detention if caught. That was part of the thrill.

So, this was how things would go during the next year, Oliver mused. He would bear it. Foremost on his mind, however, was Juan's payback no matter how long it took. Over the next month, Juan's taunting of Oliver and his crew went underground. Staff appeared not to notice and the youths who did, dared not report it. Oliver and his crew endured the continuing indignities, as they knew their day would come.

Juan never saw it coming. He'd just taken his seat to play video games with youths who, like him, had earned additional privileges. Others, like Oliver, could only play table games. When the lead officer on duty left his desk to set up the video game system, Oliver grabbed the officer's chair, ran to where Juan was seated and brought the chair down squarely on Juan's head, knocking him from his chair to the floor.

"Now who's the little bitch, my nigga!"

"You're out of here, Oliver," a staff officer barked as they pulled Oliver away from Juan. "You just brought yourself more time in our fine establishment."

"It was worth it," Oliver replied coolly, looking at Juan, as staff phoned paramedics for the still-dazed youth.

Oliver's previous judge was not happy to see him in her court the next morning. "You didn't last long at Alcatraz," she remarked.

"Just send me home. I'll do what I need to do," Oliver responded. "I'm not going back there."

"I'll make that decision, Mr. James. Well, actually, *you* made the decision. Home is where you're *not* going. I understand you want your plea hearing this morning and that you intend to admit the charge against you and be sentenced."

"That's right. I just wanna do my time and be done with all this."

"The State has done you a great favor by charging you with simple battery even though Juan

119

remains hospitalized under observation for a concussion."

"He got what was coming to him," a sullen Oliver replied.

"Counsel, you may want to caution your client," the judge suggested. "Before you dig your hole any deeper, Mr. James, do you admit the charge of battery against Juan?"

"Gladly," Oliver replied.

"Then you will serve an additional year at Alcatraz, suspended for now. If you stay out of further trouble at Alcatraz for the next eleven months, you may be released to your family. I hope you'll make progress with your high school diploma."

Don't count on it, Oliver thought.

"Next case, bailiff. Good luck, Mr. James," the judge added, as Oliver was led out of the courtroom.

Once back at Alcatraz, Oliver's "island cred" was established among the other youths. All he had to do was endure the remainder of his time there and stay out of trouble. He later learned that Juan's injuries would not allow him to return to Alcatraz and that he'd been placed in a staff-controlled group home for the last month of his sentence.

Oliver figured he could do his eleven months with little effort and trouble and thus avoid having to serve the additional year imposed by the court. School was not an option in his mind but he attended as required. After completing the eleven months with only minor infractions, Oliver was released home to his parents. But within six months, he was again arrested for tagging and returned to Alcatraz for an additional year. He would be eighteen by his release date.

"Oliver, what's up dude?" one of the detained youths called out as Oliver emerged from re-orientation at Alcatraz. "Welcome back. It's Oliver y'all! Some of you bitches are gonna have to pay up. Man, they bet you'd never come back here," continued Darien Paul, who'd been sentenced to Alcatraz just prior to Oliver's release. "But here you are! Did you hear anything about Juan while you were out?"

"Nah. I didn't hear anything about his punk ass. Besides, he definitely didn't want to see me after the beat down I gave him."

"Dude, what the hell?" staff officer Saltzman remarked as Oliver entered the main hall. "You back again? And so soon?"

"I'll do my time, man," Oliver replied. "I always do."

"Well I hope you make it count this time. You're about seventeen now, right?"

"That's right."

"Well you know what happens if you don't earn that diploma, right?"

"I know I won't be coming back here."

"Yeah, but do you think the next place will be better? That'll be prison, dude. Don't you want your freedom?"

"Only on my terms."

"Your terms keep bringing you back here."

"I'm a tagger, man. That's what I am. That's what I do. I ain't got time for the rest of this shit here. Besides, no one teaches us nothin' here."

"I'm gonna share something with you dude, in case you haven't figured it out already. No one really cares about teaching you anything here. All of the resources are in the community schools, not here. Besides, we're not trained teachers. In the community schools you could study almost anything you wanted."

"Yeah I know. Stem, stem, stem. I'm not interested in that shit man. I like to tag. They don't teach that in school."

"I'm sure you never attended long enough to find out. But the arts get more respect now dude. You taggers call all of that scritch-scratch you do in the streets art, don't you?"

"Some do. Not me. It's just taggin'."

"You're not dumb, Oliver, although Alcatraz is certainly known as the place where dumb kids live. I don't think most of you here are dumb. Well okay, *some* may be. You all just make dumb-ass decisions. Part of that is because you're still young and aren't yet playing with a full deck upstairs. In your case, however, I think you're just stubborn, defiant, and afraid."

"I ain't afraid of shit, man. You got that wrong. I ain't afraid of nothin' or no one."

"Oh, you wear that toughness like a shirt, but you're scared as hell. Morning classes are about to begin. You know the drill so line up. I think I've got your last class this afternoon. We'll continue our discussion there."

"Oh. Is that what we're havin' here?"

"I gave you too much credit earlier," Saltzman replied. "Maybe you're too dumb to figure that out."

As Oliver entered his last class later that day, Saltzman stood at the classroom door as the youths entered. The officer directed Oliver to a seat near the back.

"Take that seat right there, next to the desk with no computer screen."

"Now you're talking. Back of the classroom I can nap undisturbed."

"You know I usually don't care if you guys nap or stare out the window. I have my diploma. Just take a seat. We'll continue our "talk" after I get the class started on the afternoon lesson. I think you'll want to stay awake this time.

"All right. Everyone in a seat by the time the bell rings. If you're fortunate enough to have a desk with a computer screen, power it up to see if it's working. Those with no computer, thank yourselves, then take a seat and stand by for further instructions."

Oliver was surprised that his seat not only had an intact computer screen but a computer that worked. The three youths seated closest to him had no computer screens on their desks. It didn't appear to bother them as each put his head down on the desktop.

"Okay," Saltzman bellowed, "the bell has rung and it's time to get started. All heads up and facing front and center while I go over today's assignment. You're gonna cover three subject areas this afternoon: English, basic math, and science. Those of you with computers may log in and start with any of the three. Once you've finished one subject, you will change seats with anyone who does not have a computer so they can also work one program.

"Keep switching off until you've completed the three programs. I will check before end of class and give credit where credit has been earned. Those who do not complete all three programs will get negative points. Three of you with working computers have bonus points so you may complete all three programs before allowing someone else to use the computer. And, as you know I always reserve a working computer for the guy most resistant to change and today that desk is reserved for..."

"Oliver!" the class shouted in unison before breaking into laughter.

"As it turns out, you're right. Oliver is back from his brief stint in the community so he'll get a computer today. We'll see if he's willing to conform enough to finish his education and get out of here for good."

Oliver acknowledged the applause that followed Saltzman's remarks by bowing from his seat. Hard to believe that at seventeen, he was considered one of the OGs[11] of juvy. Other youths who began with him in the juvenile system had moved on and were back home, working toward their high school diplomas. One was headed to college.

In the six months after Oliver's release from Alcatraz the previous time, two of his tagging associates went to prison and one was killed during a drug deal. Oliver accepted that he was a serial tagger. Fortunately, his delinquency had not escalated into full-scale violence, save for taggers' skirmishes over territory. His attorney suggested to the court that Oliver's penchant for tagging might have a mental health component that needed evaluation. However, the judge ignored the attorney's argument and Oliver wanted to punch his attorney for making it. There was nothing wrong with his mind. He just had no use for education and

---

[11] Original Gangstas

was determined he could survive in the community without one.

As his fellow classmates settled into their coursework, a morning nap, or horseplay, Saltzman approached Oliver and sat down at the adjacent desk.

"I want you to watch something, Oliver."

"You know I'm not down for this crap," Oliver replied, quickly on the defensive.

"Sadly, I know that. But I suggest you make an exception for this. You've been here enough to know that only students with bonus points get to monitor live feeds from the classrooms in the community. When they do, they can take additional classes with those kids in real time. If they earn sufficient points by completing all of their course work here and bonus points by monitoring classes in the community, they can earn their diplomas quicker and in some cases, get time shaved off their sentence."

"Yeah, I know all that. So? I'm way too far behind to qualify for any of that crap."

"I'm gonna let you watch one anyway. And afterward, I want you to think." Saltzman tapped the side of Oliver's temple with his forefinger and returned to his desk to begin the live feed. It featured the previous day's completion and judging of an art contest.

Within five minutes of watching the live feed, however, Oliver became visibly agitated, tore off his

126

headset, and threw it on the ground. Without permission he left his seat and stomped over to Saltzman's desk.

"What's the big idea? What makes you think I want to watch that little bitch? You know I beat him down my first year here. He thought his taggin' was all that but he knew we were better—that *I* was way better 'n him!"

"You know I could give you three days in your cell for leaving your desk without permission. So, if you'll calmly return to your seat and finish the feed, I'll pretend you had a bad leg cramp and needed to stretch. Remember I told you that you were afraid?"

"And remember that I told you I ain't afraid of nothin'?"

"Then, if that's the case you'll have the courage to watch the rest of it."

Grudgingly, Oliver returned to his seat and resumed viewing. It appeared that Juan, the rival tagger he beat up during his first tour at Alcatraz, was about to graduate high school. He had also been named winner of his high school's tagging contest, winning a summer apprenticeship with a famous adult tagger on the East Coast and a full scholarship to a New York art school.

Oliver struggled to fight back tears as he watched the contest results. He and Juan had fallen down the delinquent chute into juvy some time ago and Juan had finally emerged out the other side. Oliver suddenly realized he'd been

127

repeating the same circle for nearly two years. It always closed at Alcatraz. How could it be that bitch ass Juan, who could not tag his way out of a barn, was about to graduate high school and attend college in New York? Oliver had never been out of his community except for his time at Alcatraz, and he could out-tag Juan on his worst day.

Of course, he'd never tell Saltzman, but Oliver had flirted with the idea of returning to school. Truth was, however, he was so far behind he knew he could not catch up.

So he pretended it didn't matter when, in reality, it did.

Especially now that Juan had found a way out. How could Oliver let anyone know he wanted to be a success when he'd made an art of failure?

Defeated by what he'd watched and his pride wounded, Oliver switched over to the day's coursework and completed it as best he could. He did not read well and his test scores from the day's assignments would reflect that. The few times Oliver attended school in the community he was too embarrassed to request help with reading, and the further he fell behind, the less interest he had in attending. Saltzman was surprised to see that Oliver had completed the day's assignments after watching the contest results. He had done poorly on each segment but had completed all three.

As Oliver and the others filed past officer Saltzman at the end of class, the officer nodded at

128

Oliver, tapping the left side of his own temple with a forefinger, a silent command to "think!"

For the rest of that day Oliver did just that. He thought about his seventeen years on the planet and how he had mismanaged them. It would be evening before he could be alone in his cell. After lights out, overcome with emotion, he stuffed as much of his sheet into his mouth as he could and sobbed for hours. He was utterly alone in the world. No real friends. The few not in prison or dead had gone straight and avoided him at all costs. His family had given up on him long ago and he was no longer welcome in the family home. His parents did not visit him at Alcatraz or accept his calls, each having served a week in jail for his recommitment to Alcatraz.

Additionally, the few acquaintances who remained no longer allowed him to crash on their sofas. As soon as the authorities discovered one of them harbored a juvenile on probation who did not attend school, that person was fined and sometimes jailed for enabling his delinquency. A dead end in front of him. Bridges burned behind him. This was the terrifying reality Oliver awakened to the next day.

After breakfast, he made his way to class with the others, wholly detached from their conversations and antics. When he observed that another student occupied the desk Saltzman reserved for him the day before, Oliver walked to an empty desk and sat quietly. Today he had no computer and the computer screens on the desks closest to his were all shattered. Saltzman quickly assigned the morning's lessons. However, a skirmish over seats at the front of the classroom erupted and one of the youths involved in the fracas picked up a chair and threw it at his adversary. Saltzman immediately intervened, ejecting the warring parties from the classroom and waiting just outside the door until staff arrived to transport the offenders.

As soon as Saltzman stepped outside the door, a snowstorm of paper missiles blanketed the classroom. In his peripheral vision, Oliver saw gang signs thrown in the aftermath of the earlier skirmish and heard the usual gang posturing comments. For once he was not a part of it. He sat in the eye of a swirling storm. Suddenly, he snapped out of his detachment and surveyed the classroom with a newly sober eye. It appeared to be a microcosm of his old neighborhood: shabby, broken, marked up, and chaotic.

"Let's have some fuckin' order in here!" Oliver declared, leaving his seat without permission.

Saltzman, still waiting just outside the classroom door with the fighters, smiled as Oliver walked to the front of the classroom.

LIBERTY OR EUCALYPTUS

The rag tag human locomotive cautiously entered the Chamber of Justice, bound not by railroad car couplings but by rough-hewn metal chains that bound each man to the other. Timothy chugged into the Chamber out of step with the human chain in front of him and took a seat.

"All rise!" the chamber agent shouted. As he rose with the others, Timothy watched as an amorphous shadow wearing black entered the courtroom and took a seat above him and the others.

"Good morning, ladies and gentlemen," came a voice from that same direction. The cheerfulness of the voice belied the darkness of the proceedings. There was nothing remotely good about this morning, Timothy mused, and it irritated him that the figure of darkness perched on the bench above him suggested it.

"How much time you lookin' at?" asked the brother-in-bondage attached to him.

"What's it to you?" Timothy replied, in no mood for pleasantries.

"Just makin' conversation, Jack. No need to be a little bitch about it."

"My name's not Jack and whether I'm a little bitch or not doesn't matter. After today, you'll probably be somebody's little bitch."

"And you won't?"

"Quiet!" the chamber agent roared in their direction.

"Not likely."

"That right? I hear this judge don't give nobody probation."

"Well we'll see, won't we?"

"Call the first case."

As the day's drama in the Chamber took center stage, Timothy remained attached to the human locomotive. His mind was not shackled, however, and it slowly backed out of the Chamber and sped away through a countryside. The murkiness that had cloaked his life like a shroud suddenly cleared, revealing what had been a life-long preparation for this moment.

Timothy had begun his twenty-year life of crime in 2030 when, after dropping out of high school, he discovered he could not compete with robots for the menial jobs he had counted on. Since he had no interest in further schooling or training, a life of crime was the next logical step. He never minded the intermittent jail terms, as they afforded a temporary respite from his illegal activities, and he always had a release date. This time, however, there was no way out. His sleeves were empty.

A soul had expired and Timothy would have to pay, but an exchange of souls was not required in his case. The People wanted something more precious—his liberty. Timothy prized his freedom above everything and everyone, even though he tested its boundaries with each new offense.

"The matter of Jonathan Kwan," the agent announced. Timothy felt a slight tug on his wrist as the human boxcar on the other side of him stood up. He'd barely noticed the man up until that point.

"Mr. Kwan do you have anything to say before the Chamber pronounces sentence?"

"I do not," Kwan replied quietly.

"Then this Chamber sentences you to twenty-five years to life."

Kwan's core suddenly hollowed as he slumped back into his seat.

Another one gone, Timothy thought, having been jolted back to the Chamber proceedings by the tug on their mutual chains.

Timothy had ignored the spectators in the chamber. He was long estranged from his family except for his daughter. And there she sat with her mother. He was happy to see his only child but furious that her mother had brought her. She was only five.

Despite his love for her, he'd been a piss poor dad. His thirst for freedom eclipsed the relationship

133

with her mother long ago. He maintained sporadic contact with his daughter as best he could when he was not in jail. When his criminal escapades proved profitable he gave the first fruits, however poisonous, to her.

"Matter of Timothy Langer."

Timothy's gaze locked on his daughter as he rose against his chains.

"Your attorney has argued for a grant of probation, which is out of the question. Do you have anything to say, Mr. Langer, before sentence is pronounced?"

"Yes."

"You may proceed."

"I would like to hug my daughter. She is present with her mother."

"What say you, agent?"

"Normally not allowed, sir."

"I will allow it this time. Mr. Langer may be uncoupled and brought out of the box. The child may then approach with her mother. I want a chamber agent on either side of them."

Now detached from the human locomotive, Timothy faced love in its purest form as he bent down to hug his daughter. She cupped his cheeks with her tiny hands.

"Are you coming home, Daddy?"

"I don't think so, sweetheart. I did something bad and I'm going to get a punishment that won't let me come home now. I'm so sorry I won't be leaving with you and Mommy today. I love you and am always thinking about you."

"The mother and child will leave the Chamber now."

Proceedings stopped until Timothy was reattached to the others and the child and her mother left the Chamber.

"Mr. Langer, you are hereby sentenced to life without the possibility of parole."

"I reject that sentence."

Timothy's attorney jumped to his feet and demanded a mental competency evaluation.

"No need," Timothy replied after his attorney's request. "I am quite competent. And I have been well counseled by my attorney. I reject the Chamber's sentence."

"Very well, Mr. Langer. I will note for the record that your rejection of sentence is made against the advice of your attorney. What is your choice?"

"I choose eucalyptus."

Moments later the chamber agent presented Timothy with an open wooden case containing several vials. Timothy nodded toward the one labeled "eucalyptus." The vial was placed in his bound hands and virtual reality goggles were placed over his eyes.

"Whenever you're ready, Mr. Langer."

Timothy raised the vial to his mouth and drank its contents, causing the human locomotives on either side of him to raise their arms along with him. Eucalyptus had always been his favorite aroma and he savored its fragrance and taste as he drank.

Once again Timothy backed out of the Chamber station.

He closed his eyes to whatever was playing inside the goggles. He preferred his own reality. He was now driving along a stretch of California road through stands of eucalyptus trees that would soon reveal the beauty of Monterey Bay. It was a very familiar scene, as he'd often driven this road during his criminal exploits.

The car windows were rolled down, allowing the cleansing fragrance from the trees to permeate the car and his being. He could not inhale deeply enough as he rounded the curve in the road which brought the Bay into full view. At this moment, the goggles were removed and Timothy was once again the center of Chamber proceedings.

"All rise," the agent called out. Timothy watched the same flash of black above him leave the Chamber as it had entered. The human locomotive also strained to rise and leave as it had entered but was unable to do so, as Timothy suddenly slumped forward. The People wanted his liberty. He gave them his soul instead.

The chamber agent slowly approached as the human chain struggled against Timothy's weight.

"One to uncouple."

SUPPORT

"You've finally earned your real man pants, Becker! Here ya go. Step forward and put 'em on!" a voice commanded from a hallway outside the day room.

A small window separating the hallway from the room where Joe Becker waited with the others quickly opened, and a pair of blue cotton slacks tossed inside landed at his feet. As he stooped to pick them up he warily eyed the other men in the room. When no one moved toward him Becker stood up, donned the pants, and walked to the picnic-style table in the center of the room, sitting down with quiet confidence.

"The rest of you diapered eunuchs need to recognize."

Some of the men, a few of them naked, turned away from Becker in shame. Others looked at him with envy. Still others looked at him in disgust. Ed Thompson in particular.

Son of a bitch, Thompson thought. *So this joker got a pair of pants. Big deal.*

But Thompson's sole wardrobe of a paper diaper was no match for the fifty-five degree temperature maintained in the day room. Nevertheless he vowed from the moment he was detained, jailed, and forced to wear a paper diaper that he would not be broken. He was a man whether he wore pants or not. He'd make *them* recognize. Especially Joe Becker.

Thompson and the others were new on the unit but Becker had been there about three months. Now that Becker had earned his pants, he would be transferred out of the unit soon, and begin preparations for his release to the community.

As Becker quietly observed the others, he focused on Thompson. Though they'd never spoken during Thompson's brief time on the unit, or even acknowledged one another, he could feel Thompson's anger toward him. He wasn't afraid of it. In the brash thirty-something Thompson, the forty-one-year-old Becker saw himself and the way he arrived on the unit. Angry. Defiant. Resistant. He knew Thompson was a tough nut, but in order to get out he'd have to crack.

"Everyone line up!" day commander Joe Belusco boomed from the hallway. "Becker, you can step out of the day room and come with me. The three newbies remain standing until staff arrives with your diapers. I don't want to see one bare ass on a seat in there unless it's wearing a diaper."

"Thompson, you and the other four line up and prepare to follow me and Becker. We're going to the room next door—you can see it through the glass window on the side wall. You'll see six tables. Find the table with your name on it and remain standing until we're ready to begin." The four men behind Thompson were also diapered.

The three men without clothes had just cleared booking following their arrest the night before. They had been relieved of everything in the process and arrived at the day room naked, totally stripped not only of clothing but also of any confidence or bravado they might have been able to muster in other circumstances. A unit officer entered the room to guard the three men and wait for the morning staff to arrive.

Becker had already stepped out into the hallway. Thompson was at the head of the line with the other four men. But he refused to move forward.

"Last chance, Thompson," Belusco called from the hallway. "Step out of the day room into the adjoining room and find your table or you're done for the day."

"Then I guess I'm done."

"Removal from day room," Belusco announced, directing his comment toward the radio on his wrist. Within seconds the day room door opened and two security guards entered, grabbed Thompson by both arms and dragged him into the hallway.

"If you assholes think working for cents an hour is going to make a man out of me, you're wrong," yelled Thompson as he was ushered out of the

139

room. "I'm already a man, dammit, and I'm not getting with this bullshit program. The little bastard can starve for all I care."

Thompson's ranting faded as he was taken from the unit back to his cell. He would be stripped of his paper diaper and placed naked on the cement floor. Like the day room, cell temperature would be maintained at fifty-five degrees. He would receive an energy bar and four jars of baby food for the remainder of the day. In the morning he would receive a paper diaper and again be transported to the day room.

The men lined up behind him may have shared Thompson's sentiments but were smart enough not to voice them. They too hated the paper diaper issued upon their arrival. They were also cold and hungry. The only way out, however, was through.

In late twenty-first century America, society had zero tolerance for parents, still mostly men, who did not support their children. The federal government had stopped funding supplemental food programs for children who had at least one parent, and many local governments were not willing to shoulder the drain on services caused by deadbeat parents.

As a result, the parents—both men and women—were jailed and forced to endure the same deprivation as the child. If the child had not eaten or did not have diapers or clothing, the parents would be similarly deprived of sufficient food and clothing until they had earned enough at the

Support Center to support the child. Men and women were detained in separate locations.

The newest men on the unit this morning had been processed into the Correctional Support Center the previous evening. A few, like Thompson, had been there one week. Each of the new admittees was provided one paper diaper for the day and sufficient nutrition to support life. They would wear a paper diaper daily until they had earned the equivalent of a month's supply of food, diapers, or clothing for their child or children. Once that was accomplished they would be issued a tee shirt. They would receive pants and be given a release date after earning three months support for their child.

Commander Belusco was a middle-aged family man who began as unit security officer when the Support Center opened a decade ago and worked his way to the top. He still enjoyed his work and tried to encourage the men who appeared amenable to change. He had no mercy on the resistant, like Thompson.

With Thompson back in his cell, the remaining men entered the adjacent room where Becker waited with Belusco.

"This is how it's gonna go while you're here," Belusco explained. "You'll have one cup of coffee or tea for breakfast and one breakfast shake with essential nutrients and energy. For lunch you'll get a bowl of soup and one jar of baby food. For dinner, two high-calorie energy bars. That's it. When your kid gets enough to eat, along with sufficient clothing, you will too. Until then, those will be your provisions. One more thing: this is not a country club so your families will not be able to put any money on your books."

The inmates' grumblings began before Belusco finished explaining. He was used to it and never acknowledged their comments.

"Any questions before we get started?"

"Yeah, dude," said one of the inmates. "Just what do we have to do?"

"Becker here will go over that with you after I'm done. However, bottom line, *dude*," replied Belusco, "is that you gotta work and feed your kid or kids. The government is no longer willing to do it for you. Real men support the children they bring into the world. Becker will be leaving the Support Center soon. He'll explain the rest. You're up Becker. Give 'em a little of your background first."

"All right then. I'll make this brief. My name is Joe Becker. I fell behind in my child support payments for seven days and panicked. I knew the weekly diaper and food supply would be exhausted so I disappeared until they caught me three months later. In that period I lost my job, of course, because I stopped going. I've been here three months and have earned my child support arrears. And, as you witnessed a few minutes ago, my pants. I got the tee shirt after the first month."

"I'm going to add in here," Belusco interrupted, "that Becker's child support obligation was only about sixty-five dollars per month, right?"

"That's right. But times three because I have three kids. The Court set it low because my income was very low but I had steady employment."

"You guys know as well as I do," Belusco continued, "that most of you will spend $65 in a week on cigarettes and beer. That's not a lot towards child support in a month, believe you me. I got four of 'em myself. However it *is* support."

"So here I am," Becker continued. "And here you are. You'll be working everyday you're here. No days off. If you had employment before coming here and that employer will allow you to return upon release, you're in good shape. But you'll still need to work at something here if that employer does not have a program onsite."

"Okay Becker, I'll take it from here," Belusco again cut in. "For those of you who need employment or seek better jobs, several local companies run programs here. They will consider you for employment after your release, depending on your ability, attitude, and work ethic.

"You can choose from gastronomy, drone repair and maintenance, robotics repair, virtual office systems maintenance, and computer programming. Any field is open to you if you have the skills, raw talent or willingness to learn. Look at the job packets on the tables in front of you. Choose one and head to the worksite for it on this floor as indicated. Good luck. What is it, Becker? You're chompin' at the bit."

"My "diapered eunuch" remark earlier was uncalled for. That's how I felt the first time I had to wear a diaper here.

"Since they're trying to make a man of me, I'll do what I think a real man would do and apologize."

"Thank you for that, Becker. All right boys, get to it," Belusco ordered.

The next morning a newly diapered but still defiant Thompson returned to the day room with the other men, including those detained the previous day. The moment he saw Becker, Thompson started to seethe. Who was this sonofabitch anyway? He just wanted to beat the hell out of him. *I'll show him,* he thought.

"Glad you're back," Becker said to Thompson.

"What's it to you?"

"It's nothing to me. But could mean a lot to you."

"None of your concern," Thompson shot back. "Those cheap ass pants make you a guru?"

"No. Let's just say they mean I'm becoming what you aren't," Becker replied coolly.

"And what's that, grandpa?"

"A man," Becker replied.

Thompson lunged at Becker and Becker drew back his fist.

"Don't do it, Becker!" Belusco commanded. "He ain't worth it."

"We'll square this later, old man," Thompson whispered.

"That we will."

"All right, Thompson," Belusco began. "Let's try this again. Step out of here into the next room so you can get started. I'll brief the new guys in the interim."

"Not doing it," Thompson replied.

"One to remove," Belusco again called for Thompson's removal. "Not wasting time with you, Thompson. You're done for today."

"Tomorrow's another day, ain't it?"

"Right you are, Scarlett. And at the rate you're going, you'll enjoy a lot of your tomorrows right here." Belusco's response triggered laughter and taunts from the others. Thompson wanted to swing on Belusco but thought better of it. Instead he cursed Becker and the other men as he was dragged back to his cell.

Later that evening after dinner, Becker requested permission to speak with Thompson before night lock up.

"Not the way you two squared off earlier today," the evening commander replied.

"I'll be outside his cell and on the way to my own. Besides, there'll be a guard watching us."

"You're already doing your work Becker and are almost out of here. You don't get extra points for being a Good Samaritan."

"Not sure there's much goodness in me. Look where I am."

"I'll give you five minutes. We certainly haven't had any luck with him. He's a pretty tough nut. Can't say I care, but have at it. I'll let staff know you're cleared."

Thompson lay shivering on his cell floor but jumped up the minute he saw Becker approach.

"What now, bitch? You want in? Or are they gonna let me out so we can finish what we started this morning? I'm not a man? Unlock this cell, guard. I'll show this joker how a real man gets down!"

"Not gonna happen, Thompson," the guard replied in a flat tone.

"A real man supports his kid," Becker said quietly.

"Well you're here, aren't you?"

"I am, but I'm about to get out. I'm a slow learner but I'm learning."

"I told you all yesterday, the little bastard can starve for all I care. My dad didn't take care of me. Neither did my mom for all that matters. Times are tough out there. I can barely take care of myself. Let alone some kid the mom won't even let me see."

"I didn't have a dad either. Most of us here probably didn't have dads. And true, some of our

146

kids' moms are nuts. But that doesn't let us off the hook."

"The little bastard has his mom. She's working. She didn't want me around so let her take care of him."

"She may not want you around but you know from your own experience that your son does."

"Yeah, but she won't let me see him. So why should I feed someone I can't even see?"

"Because he's your flesh and blood and incapable of feeding himself. Besides, you know she can't keep you from seeing him. That's just an excuse."

"Well, I don't want anything to do with either one."

"Now at least you're being honest. So you're mad at dad and your child's mom. Got anything else? Did the "little bastard"—as you call him—hurt your feelings too?"

"Why are you even here? Those pants make you God? You can just keep it movin'. I'm out," Thompson replied, turning his bare ass to Becker to once again lie down on the cement. "And don't even think about talking to me after lights out. I'll keep the whole unit awake all night if you do."

"Let's go, Becker," the guard directed. "That acorn needs to roll around on the cement a while longer. G'night, Scarlett," he chuckled as he walked Becker to the adjacent cell.

Later that evening, sometime after lights out, a quick flash of light in the corridor and the sound of a key opening a nearby cell awakened Becker.

"Wake up, Thompson. You've got company," he heard a voice say in the darkness. Becker recognized the voice as that of the night guard. Thompson did not reply.

"Thompson!" the guard shouted into the cell. "Wakeup. You've got company. Where are your manners?"

By now Thompson was partially awake but wary. He had not seen the flash of light or heard the keys. But he'd heard the guard shouting for him to wake up. In the darkness he made out a man's form outside his cell.

"I'm awake. What's going on?"

"I told you, Thompson, you have company." This time the guard quickly swept his flashlight from one side of the cell to the other. Thompson immediately caught a glimpse of what the flashlight revealed. Now fully awake he sat up, frantically scooted his back into a corner of the cell and started screaming.

"No! No! No! Stop it! Stop it! Stop it!"

There on all fours crawling towards him was his infant son.

"Take him out. Get him out! Take him out of here! Why are you doing this? He's a baby! It's too cold and dirty. And he's naked! Somebody get him out of here!"

Though he initially recoiled in horror at the sight of his son, Thompson sprang to his knees and prepared to grab his son at the next flash of light. But there was no light for the next several seconds.

"What are you doing?" he demanded. "Give me some light. You know I can't see him!"

"There he is," the guard laughed, taunting Thompson with several intermittent bursts of light that showed the infant in a different place each time.

Thompson frantically crawled around in circles, his hands sweeping the floor in front of him in the darkness.

"Help me! Give me more light. Why are you doing this?" Suddenly Thompson heard something hit the cell bars near the door and scrambled towards it. It had to be his son. But it wasn't.

It was fabric. Maybe pants. But he could not tell in the darkness and did not care. He quickly seized whatever it was with both hands. At least now he had something to warm his son with. He saw the infant in the next flash of light and lunged toward him with the fabric but again failed to make contact.

Notwithstanding his growing panic, Thompson tried to calm himself as his son started crying.

"Help me for God's sake! He's going to freeze to death in here. Help me. Get him out of here. Somebody needs to take care of him."

"It's your child, Thompson. You take care of him," the guard replied.

Now both furious and frantic, Thompson stopped turning in wild circles and stayed on his knees, fabric poised to cover the infant in the next burst of light. The opportunity came seconds later. Seeing his son directly in front of him, Thompson immediately scooped up his son in the fabric and was about to embrace him when he realized that his hands—and the fabric—were still empty. There was no question he'd grabbed his son. The infant had been right in front of him. But again he'd come up empty.

"Why are you doing this? Help me! Help him! He's just a baby!" Thompson shouted over and over, wildly sweeping the floor with his hands. Horrified that he could not find his son, Thompson again recoiled into a corner of the cell, this time howling in anguish. Defeated. His fears of being unable to protect his child a painful reality.

In the final burst of light Thompson sat motionless as a guard removed his son, now swaddled in the fabric he'd found on the cell floor. This time he heard the cell door being locked.

Thompson shivered, howled, and shrieked into the night until his wordless cries dissolved into whimpering.

The other detainees had given up hope of sleep hours earlier. The guard ignored him. As dawn approached Thompson had been quiet for nearly an hour, aside from his audible shivering on the floor.

Then he suddenly shouted at the top of his lungs, "I'm hungry. Hungry, dammit! And I'm cold!"

The guard slowly approached Thompson's cell.

"Now you know how "the little bastard" feels. See you in the day room, Thompson."

Maybe the hologram worked, the guard thought as he returned to his monitoring station. *Nothing else has.*

Later that morning, a visibly shaken and humbled Thompson eyed the other men as he filed into the day room with them. Aside from the two naked men who had been detained the previous evening, Thompson and the others—including Becker—were clothed only in paper diapers.

VISIONS FROM THE EDGE

RECYCLED

For most local residents, the weathered New England house Allen Howard walked away from that brisk November morning was a part of the town's Revolutionary and Civil War history. Little did they realize that the unassuming structure continued to channel its progressive past into the late twenty-first century.

Allen was unaware of the house's history and did not know how he'd arrived in the small Massachusetts town. His only interest was staying alive. His immediate goal was to make it out of town in order to enjoy the possibility of a future his long stay in the house had given him.

He was a stranger here, but his appearance—from a distance anyway—gave little hint of it. Dressed in a down vest, long sleeved sweater, baseball cap, and sunglasses, he appeared to be like any other local resident headed to the town's lone diner for the daily ritual of coffee and conversation. Allen planned to bypass the diner, however. His destination was the town's bus station two miles away.

In the distance, a woman approached who was similarly bundled against the cold. Allen set his face to convey a neighborly expression. But his clenched teeth smile suggested a wariness that prompted her to nod cautiously in his direction, then quicken her pace after passing him.

Allen sensed her unease, which only heightened his own. He'd do better next time, he thought, as he nodded in her direction and continued walking toward town. Was she one of them? They were here. He knew it. If he could only make it to the bus station and out of town, he had sufficient documents and cash to disappear.

He had arrived at the house under cover of darkness more than a year ago and this was his first venture outside of it since then. He'd kept up with the seasons and activities of his neighbors by sitting just out of sight of the window in his room. Although the house had an added-on enclosed back porch and a smaller open porch along one side, Allen never sat on either one. He knew there were at least three other residents in the house, but the compact one-story structure was roughly divided into quarters. He kept to his section and his own company.

The structure was believed to have housed participants in the Revolutionary War and later sheltered fugitive slaves from the South headed to Canada before and during the Civil War. Because its history was not well documented, however, it had never been opened to the public and bore no historical plaque on its exterior.

Allen's only contacts were with the elderly owners who discreetly managed the property, and a small team that arrived under cover of darkness to attend to him. A local doctor and his wife, Don and Ava Baxter, found him dumped in nearby woods while walking their dog one morning. His face was mostly gone, as was any identification. Allen's injuries were so severe he was airlifted to a hospital in a nearby town. He was later told he'd been in a coma when he arrived at the house—shot, badly beaten, and nearly dead.

Allen was not the first person the couple had found in the woods. His rescue, like that of others before him, was attributed to the couple's German Shepherd, Scout. The Baxters acquired Scout from a local breeder shortly after he was born. They were confident their sprawling property at the edge of a wooded area would afford Scout freedom to roam and explore. However, they were unprepared for the results of Scout's exploits.

Two years earlier, Scout entered the couple's bedroom at approximately 3:00 a.m. and began pulling the comforter from their bed without barking. Instantly awakened and alarmed, Don grabbed his shotgun, fearing an intruder somewhere in the house or on the property. Don's movement awakened Ava who took cover while Don quietly followed Scout downstairs. After several tense moments Don returned to the couple's bedroom and reported that the house appeared secure. He noted, however, that Scout had placed himself at the front door as Don approached and extended one paw toward him, as if indicating he should not approach.

Not one to invite trouble, Don headed to the back door instead and Scout followed. He was allowed outside briefly before Don called him back inside and secured the house.

When the couple awoke a few hours later, Scout began jumping against the front door. Ava suggested they take him on a brisk walk in the woods before they left for work.

Scout led them directly to a wounded man near death.

Over the next two years, Scout led them to many others—some deceased; others near death. The couple concluded that the rarely used woods had become an unofficial human dumping ground, likely for organized crime. The couple had been dedicated green movement devotees for years, recycling everything they could at home and work. Horrified by the human carnage discovered in their beloved woods, the couple put together a clandestine network of fellow enthusiasts to recycle what remained of any living soul they discovered whom others so obviously wanted dead.

Two questions were asked of anyone still conscious when found: whether they wanted family notified and whether they desired police involvement.

If the victim had family and/or desired police involvement, the network would arrange transport for medical care and have no further contact.

If the victim did not want police involvement and had no family, the network took over. Allen's case was not an easy one. He'd been unconscious when found and had no identification. His face was so mangled the network knew that even if he survived his injuries and gunshot wounds, it would likely never be restored to its previous appearance. In addition, Allen's finger and toe pads were badly burned. He had never given a DNA sample despite his numerous brushes with the law, but his rescuers would not know this or any other part of his history. The team decided to recycle.

As soon as Allen was stabilized in the hospital, a network caretaker posing as his relative arranged by phone for Allen's discharge to her care. From there he was secretly shuttled between a number of safe houses until he arrived at the house where he was to spend the next year, undergoing many surgeries and, hopefully, preparing for a new life.

Allen had little memory of that year at the house, only that he was in and out of consciousness and in tremendous pain much of the time, never sure of its source. He knew better than to ask questions. Someone was giving him a second chance he did not deserve.

He'd been a very bad man for much of his adolescent and adult life. There were many, if still

VISIONS FROM THE EDGE

alive, who would testify to it. It had been his job to see that they did not and he'd been thorough, if nothing else. The people he had served blindly since his teens obviously wanted him dead. His caretakers told him he was now Allen Howard. Only he knew that he had been Min-ho of South Korea.

Min-ho was born into a gang-affiliated family. Both his father and grandfather were gangsters, dealing mostly in drugs and sex trafficking. The first in his family to attend college in America, Min-ho was seen as the one who would profitably usher his family into the digital age. He became a talented criminal, hacking his way into the world's banking infrastructure to the tune of millions in only a few years.

He wanted out, but there was no getting out. The family insisted he continue his cybercrime exploits because the money enabled them to exit the violent trafficking trade. However, other individuals whose paths he'd crossed wanted him dead out of retribution or expediency. Additionally, many of the world's governments had a bounty on his head.

During his year in the house, Allen received the best face his team of underground doctors and caretakers could construct, given that his former one was blasted to bits. His caretakers told him they did not know what he looked like previously. The reconstruction was carried out in the house for several months; doctors arriving at night to piece him back together. They concluded that the rage directed at his face meant it had outlived its usefulness. They did not know his history, nor did he share it with them.

It was several months after the last surgery before Allen mustered the courage to look in the mirror. When he did he caught his breath. Min-ho was gone. He could not recognize himself or his family in the mirror. He had been handsome before, like his father and grandfather. He now had a bulbous nose, an artificial eye, slightly uneven cheekbones, and a downturned mouth. But he had no right to cry. He was alive.

He did not remember the hit or know who ordered it. His family? He did not believe they ordered it because his success had improved their lives. Of course he knew he would never see them again. Better that they believe Min-ho was dead. He should be. The fact that he was alive meant he had to chart a new course.

If he could make it out of town he planned to do just that. As Min-ho he knew more than a few of the killing and maiming fields like the one he'd been rescued from. As Allen, it was his turn to recycle. The only thing he could offer in that regard, however, was tainted: millions of dollars stashed in offshore accounts around the world. He didn't think the recipients would mind. In the end, the money had not served him well. Hopefully it could better serve others.

Just then Allen heard a car approaching slowly behind him. He did not dare turn around, even though instinct warned him his survival might depend on it. Running would be even worse. Instead, he quickened his step, as had the lady who passed him earlier. Maybe she had tipped them off.

The car slowly picked up speed until it was just behind him. No longer able to ignore the potential threat at his heels, Allen glanced quickly over his shoulder. He observed a late model black Lincoln town car with three men inside.

It hadn't worked, he thought. Panic set in followed by an eerie calm. This was it.

"Hey there. Get in!" one of the men commanded. Allen froze. For the first time in years he was not armed. He knew they surely were. There was no use running. Maybe death would be his freedom after all.

I'm not Min-ho! he wanted to scream. *I'm Allen Howard!* Although the protests rang loudly in his head, Allen had not uttered a sound. Turning slowly to face his fate, Allen locked his gaze with the men in the car. Where was the fear he'd always imagined? Had his victims experienced this kind of peace before their end? He saw the barrels of three shotguns discreetly pointed in his direction.

"Sorry, buddy," said one of the men. "We're headed to the diner for coffee and thought you were someone else. Have a good one," the man called out as the car sped off on its way into town.

160

COMMITMENT

Despite their youth, Ryan and Chloe sensed the long simmering storm finally approaching and hoped they were ready for it. Homework done, twelve-year old Ryan and nine-year-old Chloe remained in their father's study where they liked to wait for him to come home. The study was their father's first stop when he arrived and greeting him there was their ritual. The minute he entered the study, the children took turns relieving him of the worn leather briefcase that doubled as his virtual and mobile law office.

The children had grown up in the study as their father built his northern California law practice. They now earned an allowance dusting the shelves of books and legal memorabilia. Along with their father's comforting scent, the study held their security.

Chloe looked at Ryan as she heard the garage door that led into the kitchen opening. Like most evenings of late, her mother's recriminations started before their father reached the study.

"Where the hell have you been, David?" Pat demanded, as her husband entered the kitchen. "We waited dinner so long the children refused to eat. They've been waiting for you in the study ever since and refuse to get ready for bed. Where were you this time?"

Returning Chloe's glance without words, Ryan rose from his father's desk chair to close the study door. They had no interest in listening. They had heard this conversation too many times.

"I'm sorry, hon," David responded, the day's weariness in his voice. "I was in a meeting that went long and just lost track of time."

"Clearly. I've been patient, David. You know I have. But you keep trying my patience. It's going to be me and your kids or your goddamn mistress. Why the hell I've given *you* the power to choose these last few months I'll never understand. I'm not powerless. I warned you the last time. You're out of here, David. I want you out of here tonight."

"So I'm late for dinner and you want me out? I'm just late, honey, and I'm sorry. Truly sorry. Besides, I already made my choice. You know that. The affair is over. I promised you that and have not gone back on that promise. I think we need to talk this out. You've gone from zero to ninety and I didn't even know you were driving!"

"You're so full of shit, David. Even now, you just can't admit that the affair is not over. You sound like your clients who insist they're innocent when you know they're guilty."

"And you know I'm guilty? Just because I'm home late?"

"Well, coming home on time was the other promise you made. It's so obvious, David. Your chronic lateness was due to an affair. You've had a virtual practice since 2030. The main reason you started it was so we could shelter ourselves from all the violence out there and better protect our children when we decided to start a family. You haven't had an office in town for years. What other reason could there possibly be?"

"Some clients, and prospective clients, still favor face-to-face meetings. So do I, for that matter."

"I don't believe you. And I want you out."

"You expect me to tell our children we're getting a divorce?"

"I'll tell the children. Just go."

David bypassed the study as he went upstairs to pack. He'd made a horrible mistake in cheating on his wife. The short-lived affair was over but he realized Pat might never trust him again. Their therapist had warned that his wife's emotions likely would run hot and cold for a long time and he was prepared to make amends and weather the storm. It appeared, however, that Pat was done.

He could not face his children just yet. Once upstairs, he heard Pat open the door to his study.

"Your Dad's home. He'll be in to see you in a few minutes," she announced, trying to lighten the tone in her voice. "Ryan, you look so serious sitting at that big desk. But you can't convince me you're actually reading one of Daddy's law books."

"They have neat old pictures, Mom," said Chloe, perched atop a stack of books on a chair at the side of the desk. "You should see."

"I will later, honey," Pat replied, closing the study door and returning to the kitchen.

David reluctantly bypassed his study again on the way downstairs. Returning to the kitchen, he placed two packed suitcases near the door to the garage. Pat sat silently at the kitchen counter as he entered.

"I'll get the kids," David said quietly. As he opened the study door he was greeted with a happy cry of "Daddy!" from Chloe.

"Hi, Dad," said Ryan.

His heart cracking, David gently redirected the children toward the kitchen. "Your Mom and I want to talk to you about something. Come to the kitchen with me."

The cloud of doom that had hovered over the household for months followed Chloe and Ryan to the kitchen. They steeled themselves against what it meant and what they had to do.

"Your mother and I love you two very much—more than anyone or anything as a matter of fact. However, we are going to separate for a while. This means I won't be living here with you every day but will see you every week."

With tears streaming down their faces, Ryan and Chloe allowed themselves to acknowledge the suitcases sitting by the door.

"Do you have anything to ask us or say to us?"

"Yes," the children calmly responded in unison after looking to one another for confirmation.

"Go ahead," Pat replied.

"We don't *think* so," the children again responded in unison.

"I don't understand," said David.

"Mom, Dad," Chloe began, "when you got married, you promised to stay together forever and raise a family didn't you?"

"We did," Pat replied.

"You wouldn't break a promise to me would you, Daddy?"

"Of course not, princess."

"You wouldn't either would you, Mom?" asked Ryan.

"No. Of course I wouldn't."

"But you're breaking a promise to each other. Isn't that just as important? We are a family and we want us to remain a family here, together in one house."

"You two are just too young to understand," Pat replied.

"We understand Dad cheated and that you were hurt and are still mad at him," Ryan stated. The couple was stunned to hear their twelve-year-old sum up their misery in such a matter-of-fact tone.

"We hear everything, Mom, even though we don't want to," Chloe added.

"We need *you* to understand we want a whole family," Ryan continued. "So you two have to just work it out."

"It'll be better if Mom and I live apart for a while," said David.

"But it won't be good for *us*," Chloe insisted. "We'll be like all the contract kids at school and have a busted up family like they do. Me and Ryan are the only kids at school with married parents."

"Well, most people don't marry anymore," Pat replied, exchanging glances with David. "We've explained that to you before. Couples can just agree to stay together as long as they think it's a good idea. But they have to contract if they plan to have children. For at least two years. If they renew the contract often enough, sometimes that leads to marriage. But marriage the way your father and I did it, from day one, so-to-speak, is pretty rare now."

"But in your wedding movie, you and Daddy married forever didn't you, Mom?" Chloe asked.

"We did, sweetheart."

"Why?"

166

"Because we loved each other of course, wanted a family—you two—and planned to blend our lives together. Both of our parents had happy marriages and we wanted that too."

"And now you don't want us anymore?"

Pat was unable to respond.

"Of course we do," David replied for the couple.

"Dad, if you and Mom divorce, Chloe and I will sue you both," Ryan announced. "Uncle Rob said he would help us."

"Sue us? Uncle Rob? What on earth are you talking about?"

"Wait here," said Ryan, darting from the kitchen to his father's study. He returned just as quickly with a book.

"Breach of contract, Mom and Dad," said Ryan, "under which Chloe and I are third-party beneficiaries. We'll sue you both for breach."

"Where in the world did you come up with that?" asked David, surprised but inwardly proud of his children.

"This book from your study, Dad. Case of *Braemar v. Braemar*[12] from sometime in the 1800s. Uncle Rob said he might be able to argue for us that since you and mom promised to stay together and raise a family, that Chloe and I were future third-

---

[12] Braemar v. Braemar is a fictional case for purposes of this story.

party beneficiaries of that promise. If you divorce, not only would you breach your promise to each other but also your promise to us."

"That's right," Chloe added with authority. "And Uncle Rob said we might make some good presents with this case."

"Presents?" David asked.

"Yes. He said it was possible we'd make presents but didn't say what kind."

"I don't know if that was the exact word, Chloe," Ryan cautioned.

"Presents...presents. Is it possible he said you might make *precedent* with your case?" David asked his children.

"I think that's the word," Ryan replied.

"I see," said David, overcome by an unexpected loss for words.

"You fight for your clients don't you, Dad?"

"Of course, son."

"We want you to fight for us," Chloe replied. "And for our family. You too, Mom."

"If you break your promise to each other, then you break your promise to us, which you both say you'd never do," Ryan concluded.

"And we're not having it!" exclaimed Chloe, as she perched triumphantly on top of her father's suitcases.

ABOUT THE AUTHOR

Gail Curtis grew up in the Midwest and has lived in the South and on the West Coast. She presently lives in Las Vegas, Nevada. She has enjoyed careers in aviation and law and has traveled extensively around the world and the U.S. She enjoys local, regional and national theater productions, taking a variety of courses, and collecting globes and aviation memorabilia.